MW01701643

A CAREGIVER'S DIARY

By SueAnnPaige

eBook ISBN: 978-1-966373-61-2
Paperback ISBN: 978-1-966373-62-9

TABLE OF CONTENTS

PREFACE

This diary was kept as my way of coping with many unforeseen changes that were taking place in my life, my husband's life, and our marriage. We had planned for our retirement years to be happy and filled with travel plans, to spend more time visiting our children who were spread from one state to another, and to just enjoy life.

It seemed to start out as planned, but a stumble here and another there started to add up to one question, then another, and another, and another. I, in particular, noticed gradual changes in Rick that were giving me much concern as the months passed, and one year closed, with the next one offering more of the same.

The contents of this diary reflect only a part of what our daily lives looked like and samples of conversations. The comments are not meant in any way to make fun of or disrespect the man he had been, but it is my hope to enlighten my readers of what the debilitating diseases he lived with can do to one person, their family, and the lives of all those near and dear to them.

It is my intent to let others know that I understand each journey is different; no two are alike. If one example in this diary rings a bell in your memory, you will know we walked down that path together at some point. No two days were alike and could be unpredictable, surprisingly difficult, sometimes unprepared, and often times comical.

As I reminisce, those days of caregiving were sometimes the hardest and most frustrating, but I felt God was in control every step of the way. It was through my faith in God that I kept the strength to get through a lot of the hardest days and knowing which decisions were best at the time.

In all fairness to those who were involved in this journey, some names have been changed to respect their privacy.

DEDICATION

I dedicate this diary to all Caregivers who have survived their journey from beginning to end, to those who are somewhere in the middle, and to all who will some day be called upon to assume that responsibility for someone near and dear to them.

Keep your faith, stay strong, and keep smiling!

INTRODUCTION

I looked back through the years and tried to see exactly when my husband Rick started having signs of dementia. In hindsight, I noticed some minor symptoms shortly after he retired as an Aerospace Engineer. He was well-educated, with a degree in Mechanical Engineering and a Master's in Business Administration.

We met at work in Palmdale, California, back in 1984 when the B-1 Bomber Program was getting into full swing. We both worked in Engineering and had known each other for about five years before our departments were nearly next door to each other. I had promised myself that I'd never get married again and had no "eyes" for anyone! My motto was always, "All men are married until proven single!" I knew nothing about Rick except he was one of the nicest guys at work. One day, his department's personnel paperwork was inadvertently included with the department mail I received. One piece of paper caught my eye, and it was his Personal Change Status marked as "single!" So, a friendship just happened to blossom over time, and when we married at the end of 1989, I was head-over-heels in love with this man!

IT STARTED WITH

"An Invitation to Dinner"

Did you ever think that you would be
Married to a girl like me?
I never ever thought that I
Would meet the Apple of my Eye.

You're nicer than the days of Spring,
You're better than a diamond ring,
More handsome than a red Corvette,
The best a girl could ever get.

Gentle eyes so warm and brown,
Hardly ever with a frown,
A voice that always sounds so neat,
And a smile that sweeps me off my feet.

The first time that I saw you
I really had no clue,
That the spark I felt down deep inside
Would someday cease to hide.

For when I sat home all alone
And knew the fire had really grown,
I invited you to come and dine
On June thirteenth in eighty-nine.

Instantly, I knew my heart
Had not deceived me from the start,
You're all good things wrapped into one
Handsome, smart, and full of fun.

So, on this special birthday
It's appropriate to say,
"Don't know how I could love you more
On June thirteenth in ninety-four."

CHAPTER 01 | Shifting Gears

The B-1 Program that my husband and I worked on came to a close in the mid-nineties, and Rick was transferred to the C-130 program in Ft. Walton Beach, Florida. We sold our home in California, our furniture was transported via a moving van and stored in Tampa, and one car was sent via courier to Ft. Walton Beach, awaiting our arrival.

Hurricane Opal had hit the Florida panhandle shortly before we arrived with our new Ford F-150 truck and thirty-four foot, dual slideout, 5th wheel, which was going to be our full-time home. To begin with, we had reservations in an RV park in Navarre but were totally unfamiliar with the area. The scene that welcomed us to Florida was short of a war zone. The RV Park had no electricity, and tree limbs were blocking many of the campsites. Some roads were impassable, boats had washed ashore and were abandoned in parking lots, the main highway running parallel to the shoreline was completely washed out, and apartment buildings, businesses, and hotels all looked like a ghost town.

We found our car that had arrived before the hurricane transformed Ft. Walton Beach into a deserted town where most businesses were closed because of it. It was sitting outside in a storage yard, covered with a layer of mud and fallen tree limbs. Fearing for the worst and hoping for the best, the car survived with very few scars!

After several months, the highway was reopened, and we relocated to a beautiful RV resort in Santa Rosa Beach. We lived there for a little over three years and also had a house built in a retirement community called The Plantation in Leesburg near Orlando. Rick spent all week at the RV and drove down to the house on weekends while I divided my time between both places.

Living in Florida was a far cry from the desert we were accustomed to in California, with dry humidity. One never gets used to earthquakes in California, but moving to a state with high humidity and hurricanes was quite an adjustment. On one such occasion, Hurricane George was in the Gulf and headed up the coast towards Leesburg. Being alone during the week, I kept the weather radio going day and night. As it approached, I started packing the car with valuables until it could hold no more.

The next morning, I jumped in the car ahead of the hurricane, driving towards Santa Rosa Beach, only six hours away! I drove faster than the hurricane was traveling and arrived safely at my destination. But the storm wasn't over yet! It followed me up the coast and rounded the big bend towards Santa Rosa Beach, located between Panama City and Destin.

Keeping a close eye on the hurricane's path, we loaded all the valuables into the RV and hooked it up to the truck. The car was left at the site in hopes it would be safe until we returned. Trying to get ahead of all the traffic trying to evacuate the area, we traveled west towards Mobile, Alabama. Hurricane George was right behind us! We continued west until we arrived in Beaumont, Texas. It looked like George gave up the fight and made landfall in Biloxi, Mississippi. We were able to travel back to Santa Rosa Beach on I-10 using caution in certain areas. Fortunately, our new car had also weathered the storm.

When it came time for Rick to retire, he still had the option of returning back west with the Move Package Boeing had given him, or we could have stayed in Florida. Because the family was so far away from Florida, we chose to sell our house and move back west, but only as far as Utah, into a home we had purchased about a year before.

When move day arrived to leave Florida, Rick just hooked our 5th Wheel up to the truck and assumed everything was good to go. The first delay happened when he discovered the RV batteries were dead. It didn't occur to either one of us that the batteries would eventually die if the RV was plugged into electricity for three and one-half years! Once the batteries were replaced, we were on the road.

It was getting dark as we rolled down I-10 in Louisiana. He looked out his side mirror and said, "Oh, no!" A tire had blown on the driver's side of the 5th wheel. We got off the first exit, luckily found a place to park, and spent the night in Baton Rouge until we could get a new tire the next morning. There were no more problems until we traveled over the 2-lane road from Arizona to Nevada through Hoover Dam. There was a very loud noise coming from somewhere "back there," but we weren't able to stop until we arrived at the first casino parking lot in Nevada. You guessed it! We blew another tire that damaged the wheel well and its surrounding area on the opposite side of the RV. After a considerable delay and another new tire, we were back on the road and headed towards Utah. The moral of that lesson: Never drive on tires that have been sitting idle for years!

Rick no longer had a desire to pursue the hobbies he had once been passionate about. He lost interest in golf even when we now lived near a Country Club and had the opportunity to become members. While we were living in Florida, he encouraged me to buy a set of clubs and take a few lessons so I would be prepared to hit the golf courses after we retired, even though he never actively played golf after we moved from California to Florida. One of his avid golf buddies from California visited us in Florida and took him golfing once! His buddy actually accused me of not letting him golf anymore, but little did he know about the developing condition! The closest we ever got to playing golf in Utah was at a driving range, hitting a bucket of balls. Oh, and just to be fair, we went miniature-golfing a couple of times! His fishing gear also gathered dust in the garage after he took our grandson fishing one time.

This man used to be on his school golf team

and golfed in a twilight league once a week with co-workers. He went on fishing trips with other co-workers at least once a year to June Lake in California. One friend raved that a fish would gravitate to Rick's line the minute it hit the water, giving him the reputation of being the best fisherman in their crowd! Rick never gave a reason why he lost all interest in these two activities, but when he made up his mind that he did or did not want to do something, he wouldn't budge.

One of the first things to accomplish with the new house in Utah was to build a wall between the dining room and living room, thus turning the dining room into a new office area. He was meticulous in designing and building a wall that was almost as high as the ceiling. Leaving it open at the top allowed ample lighting in both rooms and a pot shelf as well. There were electrical outlets on both sides, and there was wainscoting in the office.

However, before he could get started with any projects, and since the garage had no workspace for a talented craftsman, he built his own work area that included lots of storage space.

After those projects were completed, he sat in

a chair looking out the office window for hours while I volunteered at the local hospital once a week. He had no idea what to do next and didn't express a desire to find a new adventure. The only activity we seemed to share was traveling in our RV, and there was only so much of that that we would be planning. It appeared that he seemed lost, with nothing to do and nowhere to go most days. I felt it was up to me to give him a boost and find honey-dos to keep him busy.

He had made six extremely detailed perpetual calendars while he was still working in California, which were given to five of our adult kids. I still enjoy the one he made for us and remember those good old days each time I advance the "characters" to a new month.

Since he really liked woodworking, this was a direction I encouraged him to pursue. It didn't take long before he came up with another idea to build a shed in the backyard. After weeks of hard work and sweat, his masterpiece resembled a small barn! He didn't buy a kit; that would have been too easy! He cut every 2x4 and each plywood panel to perfection. The double doors looked like authentic craftsmanship, and the red exterior with white trim made it the cutest little barn in the neighborhood!

Our new office needed a certain-sized bookcase to fit under two windows, so Rick soon got to work with measurements, plans, and drawings. It didn't take long before he completed a little oak-stained bookcase to fill that empty space under those two low windows.

Our closets consisted of bars to hang clothes and two shelves above those. He put his engineering skills to work again and designed built-ins to increase storage. We went to one of the big box stores that specialized in building materials and bought all the closet kits to assemble at home.

The kits were very heavy, but he managed to load everything into the RV for the drive home. I noticed he was just walking in circles and going nowhere, so I called to get his attention, asking what was wrong. He was disoriented and took a few minutes before coming back to earth! This was one of the first significant problems I noticed. As time went on, I recall entering the garage where he would be working, but instead of finding him in the middle of a task, he would be standing and staring. When I asked what he was doing, he would usually say, "Thinking!" I wondered at the time, after finding him just "thinking" that many times, if it was something more than a coincidence.

After some of these first projects, he was experiencing a very painful shoulder. When the pain continued to increase, he felt that he probably needed to have it checked out. He made an appointment with an orthopedic doctor and was soon scheduled for rotator cuff surgery on December 4, 2000. The rotator cuff is a group of muscles and tendons that hold the shoulder joint in place and allow you to move your arm and shoulder

The surgery was successful, but Rick was very combative coming out of the anesthetic—a side effect of anesthesia, particularly in older patients (although he was only 59 years old) where the patient becomes hyperactive or has disinhibition, crying restlessness, or mental confusion. The nurses tried to get him under control but were unsuccessful. Finally, the doctor had to get on top of Rick to prevent him from pulling his arm and damaging the repaired shoulder. It was no surprise that his blood pressure became a concern; it was too high! After three months of physical therapy, the shoulder seemed to be in good working condition.

He continued to have problems with high blood pressure, and his mother had warned me that it had always been a problem in their family; she wanted me to promise I would keep an eye on him! While going to physical therapy after surgery, he was put on his first blood pressure pill, and you would have thought it was a death sentence; it was such a blow to his ego!

I started to notice that his head would hang down when walking, basically looking at the floor. As time passed, I realized that it wasn't the way he used to walk. So, I asked why he always held his head down when he walked, and he told me it was comfortable that way.

Rick joined the Elks Lodge, where we started making new friends and occasionally volunteered in the kitchen for banquets. The Elks Lodge is a massive supporter of the Huntsman World Senior Games in St. George each year, and we were among the many members who volunteered our time for the thousands of athletes who participated in the sports during that two-week event. For about ten years, we looked forward to October, when we would devote much of our time to registration during the first week and validating team scores for bowling events during the second week.

We joined the local Methodist Church in 2001, where I supported as many activities as I could. He also helped with an activity where the church sold scripts as a fundraiser. It was somewhat of a challenge for him to learn the computer program that was already set up, which was another indication of early-onset dementia that I noticed but didn't give it a second thought at the time. Working on a computer had always been one of his many attributes, and he had been quite tech-savvy.

***

"Oh, I think I want to drive a Big Rig!" So, he thought this new adventure would be the answer. He researched what, where, when, and how much. Then he gave me every reason why he should and could do this. He didn't stop until I gave him a thumbs-up!

I was aware that when he wanted something bad enough, he knew how to get it! This was not a new habit; I'm sure it was a trait he had learned at a very young age, and it still seemed to work!

He drove to the Tech School one hour each way, five days a week, for at least six weeks. He was so excited about this new career after passing his academic tests, driving skills, and a physical exam. He didn't pass the first physical due to too much sugar in his urine but was told to return in a couple of days after drinking lots of water, and he passed the second time!

My one concern about the responsibilities this job would expect of him was keeping track of paperwork, which was not one of his strong attributes! Then, he went to work for a large trucking company in Salt Lake City to continue his eight weeks of hands-on schooling, which meant he drove with an experienced driver on actual trips from SLC to Las Vegas. He was gone during the week but was usually home on weekends, so we put our RV in a SLC location where he could spend his downtime during the week. In addition to the Tech School's cost, he would need special work clothes and supplies when he started driving solo.

When he qualified to do solo driving, he applied for a job with a local trucking company and was hired. He informed me that now he could be gone weeks at a time and sometimes might get home late at night, so he bought a used truck.

An engineer gone trucker
What a gutsy thing you've done,
To start a new career again
When retirement was fun.

You've learned the many dos and don'ts
In backing up and shifting gears,
The regulations of the road
While cruising through these golden years.

Now you're going to hit the road
As you grip that steering wheel,
Sitting in that semi-truck
What a thrill that you must feel!

Don't forget to watch the road!
Don't forget to stay awake!
Don't forget that heavy load!
Don't forget which route to take!

I pray the Lord will keep you safe
And be with you in every way,
I pray that He will ride with you
And give you guidance every day.

The first job, he was called to take a load to Las Vegas on Halloween night in 2004! He stopped at the local truck weigh station before leaving town and was held up for hours to re-shift the load in his trailer. For

The local Lodge was in the process of being built when he became WM, so meetings were held in a banquet room at a local hotel. Before each meeting, we were hosts for members and their ladies to attend a full-course dinner in our home. While I did all the cooking, Rick set up tables and chairs to accommodate those who had made reservations. When the men left afterward for their meeting at the hotel, some ladies stayed for a social! A small donation was accepted for each dinner that went towards the building fund.

One year, he drove us to Salt Lake City for a weekend of Masonic events. Everyone stayed at the same hotel. We were in Room 815, and our friends were in Room 220. Rick got very confused and became argumentative with me when he kept insisting our friends were on the twenty-second floor while I was trying to explain that there were only nine floors in the hotel!

Memorizing his work became more challenging during those seven years. He became frustrated and started to lose confidence, but with the Grace of God, he always met his goal! Where he might have been weak in some areas, he made up in others. Rick was a good man, polite, respectful, intelligent, and charming. Everyone liked him! Family and friends were not yet aware that he was, and had been, having a private struggle!

One evening, he was getting ready for a Masonic meeting wearing his dress slacks, sports coat, white shirt, and tie. He had worn ties all of his career, but this one night, he couldn't remember how to tie it! He later practiced and practiced but was never able to master the art again!

The year 2009 was like a yo-yo life trying to keep up with him while he was WM. After one of the dinners at our house, he had collected the money but never turned it in. He was asked about it, but he couldn't recollect what he'd done with it. The day he found the money, I asked why he had put it where he had, and he yelled, "Take me to the hospital!"

He lost the key to the Lodge one time and said he had loaned it to someone, but I don't believe he could recall who that person was. The key was later found in his coat pocket!

When his one-year term as WM was coming to a close in December 2009, I started keeping more notes because:

(1) I knew he was having memory problems,

(2) I needed documentation,

(3) I knew I wasn't imagining his deficit, and

(4) I knew I was eventually going to need lots of help!

His involvement in the Masons had become the top priority. I took photos of every activity and compiled a scrapbook that holds many fond memories to this day. Being a Mason was his biggest accomplishment and the most rewarding achievement after he retired!

***

Back in 2005, there were enough questionable concerns I had that prompted me to write a note to our family doctor before one of Rick's appointments in hopes he could give some advice if this was early stages of dementia. I mentioned that Rick had had Bell's palsy in 1997 and had noticed some changes afterward that didn't seem significant at the time but might be related to signs I was seeing now.

In 1997, at the age of fifty-six, he had been overly tired after cutting wood and pounding nails in the garage of our new home in Leesburg, FL. As he installed the new shelves in the garage, his neck had been in an awkward position. His eyes looked somewhat puffy and a little droopy, but his temperature was normal, and he was taking all his vitamins.

He called me from work after lunch one day when we were both up in Santa Rosa Beach and said the left side of his face felt like it had been given a shot of novocaine. I called our doctor and got him in to see her right after work. As soon as she looked at him, she said, "You have Bell's palsy!"

She explained that it was a virus that hit the seventh cranial motor nerve and extended to the fifth facial sensory nerve. He was given Methylprednisolone for six days and had significantly improved two weeks later when he had a follow-up appointment.

In 2005, after I mentioned Bell's palsy, his doctor said that he couldn't do anything unless a specific incident happened that would warrant Rick to be tested. He also tried to pass the symptoms off as just A-Fib. This doctor eventually retired, suffered from dementia himself, and passed away long before Rick.

I noticed that when Rick overexerted, he

would get out of breath, stop, and put his head down monetarily. When I asked why, he said he would get dizzy. In retrospect, maybe that was caused by his A-Fib!

Rick's middle daughter and her family of five came to visit us for several days, and their youngest had grown to be a little toddler from the baby she had been when we had last seen her. When Rick and I went outside to greet them as they got out of their car, he reached over and said, "What a cute little guy!"

We seemed to disagree on trivial matters as time went on. I started to feel frustrated trying to figure out what started a debate that ended up in an argument over nothing! Consequently, I started to feel unloved, unwanted, and unappreciated. Then, a new tomorrow would come, and it would be a fresh, new day. I continued to live for those refreshing days!

In the meantime, I felt his driving skills had gone south. He scared me quite a few times when he would pull out in front of an oncoming car. When he would come to a stop sign, he'd look left, right, and turn. His reflexes were getting slower, so by the time he turned, a car was coming from the direction he had first looked. I told him more than once that if he caused an accident and got me killed, I'd come back and haunt him!

I could be sitting right next to him and ask a question. I would wait for an answer, hear nothing, ask again, and he would reply that he had said……. He had said nothing! Or, I would ask him something, and his response would be totally unrelated to the question. Or, I would say something, and he would contradict me and proceed to tell me his version. In many cases, he would say exactly what I had said, except in his own words.

I started to wonder if he just wanted to argue. He had never been on a school debate team, but I sure thought he would have been good at it. I had never known him to be argumentative before. If anything, he was always more agreeable than not.

Now, if a group of people were talking about a subject he wasn't interested in, he would simply ask an unrelated question and go off in a different direction with the conversation. It was also embarrassing a lot of times when our visitors mentioned they should be going, and the next thing he did was rudely agree and practically escort them out the door!

CHAPTER 02 | Destination Unknown

Sometime during 2007, Rick was diagnosed with diabetes. He didn't take the diagnosis too seriously, simply accepting the prescribed pill with a casual "That will take care of the problem!" Rick loved food, and he truly lived to eat! Even though I did my best to prepare balanced meals, we still ate out frequently. To him, restaurant menus were like a blank check, and a buffet was nothing short of Heaven! Whenever I tried to offer advice or make suggestions, he resented what he heard as interference. Yet, despite everything, his A1c levels always seemed to be within the normal range. If that was enough to satisfy the doctor, then why did I feel it was still my burden to bear?

Rick's weight was always a challenge to keep under control. He tried every diet under the sun to shed those extra pounds, but they always found their way back to him! Given all the weight he had lost over the years and the countless diets he had tried, you'd think he would have become an expert by now. But his idea of a diet was having everything weighed and measured for him. If he wasn't following a commercial diet plan, it was up to me to plan, prepare, measure, and serve his meals.

During his busy Masonic schedule, the cardiologist continued to monitor his A-Fib. One EKG in 2007 showed no A-Fib, giving us a brief sense of relief, but another in 2008 proved that relief was premature. He was started on the blood thinner Warfarin, and we began the routine of Protime testing, a blood test that measures how long it takes for a sample to clot.

Even while we were still taking RV trips, Rick had a checklist memorized for getting either the trailer or motorhome ready for the road. In December 2009, as he started to drive the truck and trailer down the RV drive, I suddenly heard a loud noise. He had forgotten to remove the blocks from under the trailer tongue. Ouch! It was a painful reminder that things were beginning to slip through the cracks.

The propane tanks became another issue. Rick had always been diligent about checking them, making sure to get one filled as soon as it emptied. But one day, he discovered that both tanks were completely empty! It was so unlike him, and it left me feeling uneasy.

Then there was the time he couldn't figure out how to hook up the new RV batteries he had just purchased. We ended up driving through a local RV park and found someone who owned the same make RV as ours. Rick asked if he could take a look at their batteries so he'd know how to install ours. Then, he went back to the battery store to examine the old batteries again. Why? This simple task had turned into a huge challenge for him, and it felt like a wild-goose chase to me!

As we began taking RV trips less frequently, the Ford F-150 sat idle in the RV driveway for longer periods. One day, Rick decided to jump in and go somewhere, only to find that the battery was dead. Suddenly, even finding the jumper cables and hooking them up to charge the battery became a monumental task—something that would have been a no-brainer for him in the past.

This was a confusing time for both of us, leaving me to wonder whether he was doing things accidentally or deliberately. I hated to cause a conflict by mentioning these sometimes "stupid" incidents, but there were simply too many not to notice.

Rick only went to the barber once after we

were married. From then on, I took on the task of cutting his hair and trimming all the surrounding areas except for his mustache. He was able to keep his mustache and nails trimmed until a major event occurred, and then those tasks were added to my ever-growing list of responsibilities.

One time, while he was getting groomed, I asked if he had cleaned his ears. He confidently said he had, so I asked, "With what?" He replied, "With a washcloth." Well, since I knew he never used a washcloth, I couldn't help but wonder if he had used mine! After a moment, he grabbed a Q-tip and cleaned them properly. Clearly, he hadn't cleaned them before, and thank goodness he hadn't used my washcloth!

This incident is just one example of why I didn't always know whether to believe him. Over time, I found myself silently questioning his truthfulness on many occasions. Sometimes, I already knew the truth before he spoke, and other times, what he said didn't match what I knew. I began to suspect that this was a trait he had learned as a youngster, a habit that was becoming more evident as he slowly slipped back into the behaviors of childhood.

As Christmas approached, I showed Rick a new grater I had bought for myself. Guess what he bought me for Christmas? Another grater! It was one of those moments that made me smile, even though it highlighted how much he was slipping.

Rick was still able to drive, and I was still able to spend some time with my daughter Beth and granddaughter Kari in Las Vegas. Spending a week visiting them gave both Rick and me a refreshing break from our increasingly unpredictable lives.

However, while I was away, I couldn't help but worry about whether he was really doing okay. My concerns grew after I once found two spoons in the garbage disposal when I returned home. It made me wonder what else might have happened while I was gone. Whenever I called to check in and asked what he was doing, he would give me vague answers like "just messin' around," never offering any specifics. If I asked about the mail, most of the time he would say he hadn't checked it yet. By evening, I think he had just forgotten to look.

Being an avid coffee drinker, Rick usually made himself a pot of coffee every morning.

But one time, when I asked if he had made coffee, he said he hadn't because he couldn't remember how many "cups" to use! It was such a small thing, yet it felt like a glaring sign of what was happening.

***

The year 2010 approached with no hint of the challenges ahead. Of course, Rick's driving continued to be questionable, but you'd never get him to admit it. I can't remember exactly where we were headed one day, but he was driving and seemed more intrigued by the scenery than by the road. It was such a scary ride that I took over the driving, though not without resistance from him! I let him enjoy the rest of the scenery while I drove the rest of the way!

He was also doing odd jobs around the yard, and one day, he decided to cut a big limb off a tree. He just started sawing away, so I asked where he planned for it to fall. He hadn't planned anything and simply said, "Anywhere!" And anywhere it fell! Normally, the next task after cutting it up for the fireplace would have been to leave it on the RV pad to dry out, but instead, he stacked it up under the patio. In the end, it was moved to the RV pad!

Another time, I discovered some loose prescription pills in the cupboard. Rick was in charge of managing his own medications and checking his blood sugar every morning, so I was unaware he wasn't taking that particular pill. When I asked him about it, he said it was okay not to take the pill if his blood sugar was low enough. His answer made no sense, as it wasn't even a diabetic pill.

Then there were the plumbing issues. One day, I went into his bathroom to clean it and discovered a mess in the toilet. I needed him to get the plunger, but he denied having clogged the toilet, insisting that it had flushed fine the last time he used it. Guess what? No one else had used his bathroom!

I made a note to myself: "*He seems to be bored with nothing to do. Claims he's been busy today. Yes, he changed two lightbulbs, took the dog out, sat around, and fed the dog. He just loiters and watches me work in the kitchen. Wants to be called for his meals but doesn't want to help prepare anything. He has no ambition. Asks silly questions about whether he should do something instead of just deciding to do it.*"

Hygiene issues continued, like brushing his

teeth. Instead, he would just rinse with Scope. If he had brushed, the toothbrush would still be wet! I learned to go behind him to check on these things and not take his word for it. After he got an electric toothbrush, I knew whether he had brushed because it would be on the charger with the green light blinking if he had. Caught again! When confronted, he retracted his "Yes, I brushed" and finally admitted, "Oh, you're right. I only used a flossing pick."

One of Rick's favorite sandwiches was peanut butter and jelly, and he knew how to make his own when he was hungry. Otherwise, you'd rarely see him in the kitchen preparing anything. His famous quote was: "I don't like to cook, I don't want to cook, and I'm not going to cook!" One night, he fixed himself a sandwich before going to bed, but he didn't clean up the mess afterward. It was waiting for me the next morning when I entered the kitchen—crumbs on the counter and even the TV remote covered in jelly!

Another issue that became increasingly evident was his confusion between left and right while driving. His processing skills were deteriorating, and giving him directions became more of a challenge. I would tell him to turn left, and he'd change lanes to turn right. Or when he should have turned right to reach his destination, he would get in the left lane instead, always ending up several blocks out of the way.

One day, I asked if he was having a boring day, and he cheerfully responded, "Not at all." When I followed up by asking if he was happy doing what he was doing, he replied, "Very much so!" There were chores that needed to be done, but he wasn't making any attempt to do them. After drying his hands, he threw the towel over the rack instead of folding it neatly. To me, he seemed a bit rebellious that day.

Rick was passionate about trains and decided he wanted to build a layout for an H-O model. This new project came after his truck-driving adventure, and he poured countless hours into designing it. After completing the design, he dedicated an entire room in the house to the "train" room. Yes, it was that big! But after the first layout was well into construction, he wasn't satisfied and tore it apart. I can't even begin to tell you how much he invested in materials and accessories. He tore the second layout apart as well and started on a third one. Eventually, he became discouraged and left the project sitting in the "train" room for months without showing any interest. He finally sold the layout to a member of the local train club, who promised to finish what Rick had started. To hear Rick tell the story later, he was proud of all the layouts he had built and sold!

Rick had always loved to paint, whether it was creating watercolor art, applying a new finish to an old surface, or bringing life back into a dull room. He had always taken pride in his steady hand and attention to detail. But in 2010, after he painted a couple of areas in the house, it was sad to see the results. The edges spilled into the adjacent wall color or onto the wallpaper. Trying to clean up the mistakes only made them worse, and I could tell he sensed that his painting skills weren't what they used to be. He had no desire to pick up another paintbrush, but that didn't mean I wouldn't offer him a brush in the future!

We were going to one of his appointments, and as usual, I told him what our schedule was for the day, sometimes even for the next day as well. Yet, about half an hour before we were supposed to leave, he had forgotten and wanted to know who we were going to see. His memory was definitely getting worse, and it was heartbreaking to watch.

One day, someone asked me for directions, and I was in the middle of explaining when Rick interrupted and took over the conversation. Rather than cause a scene, I fumed inside and later asked if I had been giving the directions incorrectly. He said he was just trying to help, but I found it rude and didn't appreciate that he had interrupted me in the first place.

Our neighbors went on vacation and asked Rick to feed their cats while they were gone. One late afternoon, when they called to check on the cats, Rick suddenly remembered that he needed to get dressed and go feed them! The cats survived, and thankfully, they never tattled that their meals were never on time.

I did all the preparation work for our taxes each year, but we both attended the tax appointment. Our tax preparer asked a question about our pension checks being taxable, and Rick spoke up, obviously confused and not realizing our retirement checks and pension checks were one and the same. I knew he wanted to come across as being "in-the-know," but it was becoming somewhat obvious to others that he wasn't always on the right track.

Another birthday rolled around for me. I didn't hear the usual questions I'd received on all the birthdays before, like, "What would you like for your birthday?" or "What would you like to do for your birthday?" I stayed painfully quiet until that evening around seven o'clock. Then I gently reminded him that it was my birthday. He was surprised and, I think, a little embarrassed! It was hurtful for me, but I realized that at this stage of his dementia, he wasn't in control anymore. Forgetting my birthday, our anniversary, and other meaningful holidays was completely out of character for him. Celebrating any of these occasions was probably a thing of the past if it were left up to him, except…

…when it was his birthday. I bought him an ice cream cake, and he took it from me with a happy smile, carefully placing it in the refrigerator instead of the freezer! Rick loved all celebrations and wanted to be at the center of every party. I learned not to tell him secrets anymore because he would make a big announcement at the most inappropriate times. He loved to broadcast a news flash! He was thrilled to always have gifts to open—the more, the merrier! As the years passed, his celebrations became our reason to keep giving. They brought him laughter, fun, family, food, cake, ice cream, balloons, and lots of presents to open.

I learned that cell phones were becoming more difficult for him to manage. We received a message from one of his daughters, and I gave him the phone to listen to it. He listened to her message, as well as a sweet one from another daughter's son. Then, I dialed the daughter who had left the message so he could talk to her. He thanked her for her son's sweet message, but the grandson who had left the message was not her son! It was a small but telling mix-up.

I had spent a few days in Las Vegas, and Rick seemed exceptionally happy to see me when I returned home a little earlier than expected on a Thursday. I found his bed unmade, something he usually took care of every morning. He helped unpack my icebox, told me about some mail that had arrived, and asked if I'd like to go to the Tanner Theater the next night to see the Dixie Symphony. Later, I found the sugar, dry creamer, and fiber canister in the refrigerator! An announcement had also arrived from a friend, and Rick told me it was an invitation to her graduation. The Southwest Symphony, not the Dixie Symphony, was going to be at the Tanner Theater on Saturday night, not Friday night. No harm done, but the facts were not exactly accurate!

Rick was always willing to help when I mopped and waxed the wooden floors, but it never occurred to him that he could get the supplies out and do the job himself, which he was still capable of doing at that time. That would have really helped me if he had just taken the initiative! He asked questions like, "Do I pour the wax or spray it?" and "Which pad should I put on the mop?" He would offer to vacuum, but only after I had already started doing it myself. Basically, I had to supervise if he did any of the work!

It was early December 2010 when Rick got up one morning and complained that he had wavy lines in his left eye. After questioning him about these symptoms, he admitted that his vision had been bothering him for several months! Months? I knew it was time to get him to a doctor, but he insisted, "No, I don't need a doctor!"

We happened to be walking through the local mall during the holiday season, and I said,

"Let's go into LensCrafters and see if you can get a quick eye exam." Surprisingly, he agreed! The doctor saw a blank or dark spot in his eye and referred him to a specialist. Five days later, we were in Las Vegas for the first of many visits with a retina specialist, who also came to St. George twice a month to see patients, making the appointments more convenient. Rick was diagnosed with wet macular degeneration, and his eye was still bleeding. For the next eight years, he received injections in that eye every four to five weeks.

***

I started 2011 with a note to myself:

"I am going out of my mind trying to figure out what's going through his head. More and more things happen each day that drop my lower jar, speechless. Sometimes, I can't figure out his logic, his choice of words, or the way he mumbles to himself. I never know if he's talking to me. I'm convinced he doesn't care if anybody is around because it seems like he's usually just thinking out loud. For instance:

Yesterday, I told him that something was wrong with the sliding glass door—it was getting way too hard for me to open and close. His response was, 'Oh, it's just the screen door causing it.' Today, he finally took a look at it and realized he couldn't fix it, so he called a glass company. Fortunately, they worked us into their schedule and came right over. It turned out the rollers were dirty and sticking. When they left, everything worked great!

The other night, I saw something on the edge of the carpet beneath the bow window and couldn't quite figure out what it was from where I was sitting, so I asked him to come and take a look. He said, 'Oh, I saw that the other day. If it's still there, then it's dead.' So, he came over and, with his knife, pried out a dead scorpion!

A couple of days ago, I sent him to the store with a list. We always buy the 'no sugar added' Great Value applesauce, but he came home with the regular kind. I didn't realize I had to specify which kind to buy! I also wrote 'dill chips' on the list, and he came back with dill stackers instead.

I couldn't attend the new airport dedication because I wasn't feeling well, so that morning, he told me he wouldn't go either. But then, around one-forty in the afternoon, he suddenly decided to go. He left at two-ten, even though the dedication was at two-thirty, and he ended up missing it because of all the traffic!

He was asked to help with some Lodge business, and he immediately signed up for three Saturdays and some Wednesdays in between. It didn't seem to matter to him whether our schedule was already full. If someone asked him to volunteer, he would just say 'yes' without even checking the calendar first. If we already had plans for that day, then he would have to go back and rearrange everything!"

One evening, about dusk, we were walking into our local Michael's Craft Store when Rick tripped on the curb and slammed face-first into the sidewalk. The impact was so severe that it bent his glasses, which were found several feet away from where he fell. He ended up with a huge contusion on his forehead and a deep cut on his hand. Whatever we were planning to buy in the store quickly became irrelevant as we hurried back to the car. The hospital was just a block up the street, and I felt he needed to go to the ER, but he yelled that he wasn't going to the hospital and told me under no uncertain terms to take him home. So, home we went, and better he got after pouring peroxide on his bleeding hand and applying ice to his head. Later, he admitted that the cut on his hand was probably deep enough to have required stitches. Thankfully, his forehead looked better after a few days, and his glasses survived after a trip to get them adjusted.

I spent another week in Las Vegas at Beth's house, helping out where I could and spending quality time with Kari, who was in high school at the time. She and I went to the movies, shopped for any and everything, ate at our favorite tea room located inside an antique store, and enjoyed each other's company at many other food spots. Our one-on-one time created a bond that we share to this day.

Two of Kari's activities in high school were orchestra and theater. Since I was already visiting when one of her theater performances was scheduled for a Friday night, Rick drove his truck to Las Vegas to join us. The following morning, we were both gathering up our belongings, including our little Yorkie Kurly Q, to drive home in our separate vehicles. Suddenly, I experienced a medical emergency—a severe heaviness deep within my chest. I could feel it in my back, but rubbing it made no difference. Before long, I couldn't hold my head upright, and I managed to push the words out, "I wonder if I'm having a heart attack."

Rick was quick to suggest that we go to the hospital for me to get checked out. Realizing that I wasn't getting any better, I had to give in and agree. Beth drove us to the local hospital that Saturday morning, getting me there within an hour of my first symptoms. Once there, they admitted me for a heart attack.

Three days later, I was discharged, now in recovery mode, after a heart procedure to address a ninety-five percent blocked artery and the placement of one stent, followed by cardiac rehab at the hospital in St. George. It wasn't the break I had planned for or wanted, but our life definitely came to a screeching halt with no other choice. I was fortunate that Rick could drive and take care of things I couldn't manage; even though he may not have done them exactly my way, I was amazed to see how well he stepped up to the plate and was there for me!

***

The grandson of the couple who originally built our home back in 1986 stopped out front in his dazzling red sports car. After sitting in his car taking pictures of our house, I went outside, approached him, and asked if there was something I could help him with. He had enough right answers, so I believed he was who he said he was. He explained that his grandparents had built the house and that he had spent a lot of time there when he was younger.

Rick was casually retelling the story of that young man in the red sports car to someone else sometime later. As I listened, he was changing all the facts into his own version, as though he had been the one out there involved in the conversation!

This year proved that his driving skills were continuing to deteriorate. It wasn't uncommon for him to tailgate someone and then have to slam on his brakes to avoid an accident; or, if he wanted to pull into the next lane, he'd wait for a car to pass, then pull in so close behind that he could have hit the car if it had slowed down. He almost caused an accident on the roundabout near our home, and I came unglued. He said he was just trying to scare the other driver and seemed proud of what he had done!

While balancing the checkbook, I discovered I had no receipts for a couple of charges he had made. He didn't know what he did with them, so I had to remind him once again to give me all the receipts in the future. He acknowledged me with an "OK" as if it was the first time he knew I needed them!

***

With every year that rolled around, I couldn't imagine things getting any worse—and 2012 was no exception.

The injections in Rick's left eye continued every four to five weeks. Later in September, we changed retina doctors to another specialist new to St. George.

One Sunday in early January, I got ready for church as usual. Rick, however, didn't dress for church and said he didn't know we were going, even though he could clearly see I was dressed in my Sunday clothes. It was as if he didn't know what day of the week it was!

Later that day, he unloaded the dishwasher and asked where the bacon cooker belonged. I told him it went in the same place it had for the last thirteen years! Most of the time, he would just open a cupboard or drawer and toss something in there to get it out of sight. But at least he asked that time! He was the only one who drank the orange juice I bought from the frozen food section, so he had always known to take a new one out of the freezer to defrost when the container in the fridge was empty. One morning, he used the last of the OJ but didn't think to get another one out of the freezer until he wanted some the next day. It wasn't a big deal, but just another small example of his increasing forgetfulness.

Loading the dishwasher became an issue, probably because of his eyesight, and it frustrated him when he broke a plate. I could see that he was becoming more irritated as his disabilities seemed to worsen over time. I got perturbed when he quickly put a dirty dish into the dishwasher just as I was taking clean ones out. Another ongoing problem was him not looking at the "clean or dirty" sign on the door; he would open it and load a dirty dish when all the dishes were clean!

We bought two new cell phone chargers for our cars. Rick took one for his truck and left the other on the washing machine for me to put in my car. The next day, I noticed two chargers on the washer that were not in their boxes. I took one to my car and found a new one there, still in the box. Hmmm? Rick was working in the garage, so I asked if the ones on the washer were the old ones, and he said they were. I asked why he didn't just throw them away, and he yelled that he didn't know what I wanted him to do with them. Then he opened the car door, took the charger, and threw it across the garage. He later apologized for that behavior.

One of our friends was in a local rehab facility recovering from surgery, and we were going to visit her. Rick was clearly driving toward another facility, judging by the direction he was headed. When I finally spoke up to let him know he was going the wrong way, he made a quick turn at the next street. Then, it seemed he was about to miss the driveway to the entrance, so I said, "This is it!" He turned without slowing down and almost hit the curb. He said, "Sorry." I won't even say what I was thinking!

Then, on another day, I asked if he wanted to go to Rite Aid with me. Of course, he was always ready to go somewhere and still got in the driver's seat behind the steering wheel. But he headed straight for Walgreens instead! This wasn't the first time he'd gotten confused about where we were going, and he actually admitted that he didn't know where Rite Aid was, even though we had lived in the same town for thirteen years!

For some reason, I had been keeping old newspapers, but they suddenly disappeared. Rick said he didn't know where they were, so I asked point blank if he had thrown them away. He said, "I don't know." I wanted the truth and pressed, "Just tell me the truth!" He replied, "I DON'T REMEMBER WHAT I DID WITH THEM!"

While watching FOX News one day, I mentioned that the anchorman looked sick, and Rick said it was just the way his hair was combed. Huh? I thought that was a stupid answer, so I looked up some information on the Internet and read Rick some comments about him. Then he made an excuse, saying he thought I was talking about our dog!

Rick seemed bored again, so I thought I'd spark some interest in having him learn a few things in the kitchen. Since he lived to eat, I figured learning to cook might coincide with his favorite pastime! I handed him a skillet and told him to heat it up. Well, he did exactly what I told him to do—he turned the fire on high until the skillet was smoking like a chimney and then asked me if it was hot enough!

After the smoking skillet was carefully removed from the stove and a few heated words were exchanged, Rick was fired from that job! He made it clear, once again, that he didn't like to cook, didn't want to cook, and wasn't going to cook! He knew exactly how to achieve what he wanted. I was convinced that if he didn't want to do something, he didn't do it well.

Everyone probably has a list of computer passwords somewhere, right? Well, back when Rick was struggling to keep up with his computer, he asked me for a copy of my passwords. He had been computer-savvy in his good days, but I was learning the hard way that most of his knowledge had gone south. He crawled under his desk to plug in and unplug every cord, switching them around to the point where we had to call an expert in to straighten out the mess—not once, but twice! Sometime during all these fixes, I discovered my password list posted on his bulletin board, so I put it in a drawer and advised him that it needed to be kept in a safe place!

Whenever someone came to visit, Rick loved engaging in conversations and could go on and on. One such visitor was told we had moved to St. George in 1990 when, in fact, we arrived in 1999! Again, I recognized his memory was failing.

One day, I heard a terrible noise outside, looked out the living room window, and saw a huge cloud of dust coming from our neighbor's yard across the street. As the dust cleared, I saw a car coming to a stop very close to their house after careening off the road and spinning out of control! The driver had inadvertently taken her eyes off the road and lost control, with her brother in the passenger seat. I picked up my cell phone and told Rick to run over to see if they were okay. He just stood there, staring out the window, not moving! I called 9-1-1 and ran out the door! Thankfully, the two teens in the car were shaken but not seriously hurt.

We found ourselves in the local ER one weekend in July after Rick discovered blood in his urine. This was followed by a visit to the cardiologist the following Monday. The doctor decided to stop the Pradaxa Rick was currently taking for his A-Fib because there was no antidote for bleeding, whereas Warfarin had one. However, Rick had already tried Warfarin in the past. So, he was started on Xarelto, which he seemed to tolerate at the time.

After seeing the same cardiologist since 2005 for his A-Fib, we decided to switch him to my cardiologist. But it wasn't that easy once you were established with one doctor. The timing for this change was perfect since his current doctor was now only at the hospital part-time, making the transfer easier for us. I assumed Rick could fill out the lengthy questionnaire, but I quickly realized it was not an easy task for him. Several of his answers were totally off the wall, so I made the corrections and took over all future paperwork from then on! It seemed like every job I did was just one less thing for him to worry about. However, I know he appreciated my help in answering all the questions with the information and dates he could no longer remember.

With a new cardiologist, it was like starting over—with an EKG, stress test, and wearing a monitor. Of course, he was still diagnosed with A-Fib! We had the utmost confidence in my cardiologist, and it was his professional opinion that trying to surgically fix Rick's out-of-sync heart would be useless after he had been in A-Fib for so many years. Rick had had an EKG in the mid-nineties before we left California that came back as abnormal, but there had been no follow-up appointment to determine what "abnormal" meant!

I was aware that Rick said whatever came to his mind in a flash instead of knowing all the facts first. Sometimes, he would use one word when he meant another. So, when I tried to follow what he actually said instead of what he really meant, my thoughts would go off in the wrong direction.

Our communication was badly in need of help, and it wasn't good for either one of us. It was time to sit down with a serious conversation and find some kind of solution as to how we were going to face this problem together. He didn't feel he had a physical problem and thought he might need a psychologist or maybe was just getting old. He admitted that he didn't feel like doing anything anymore, and his mood was extremely low. He felt that he could never please me anymore, so he was spending more time at his computer, watching TV, reading, or eating. Most of the time, he sat doing very little.

I suggested we talk to our doctor about this problem. Maybe he could prescribe something that would help or rule out a problem. Rick agreed!

The next day, I felt like a big load had been lifted off my shoulders after he agreed to have me make an appointment with our doctor and somewhat admit there was something going on instead of being in total denial. In the past, he had said he didn't think he had a problem, so this was progress.

He seemed in a better mood, too. A couple of days later, he hadn't even taken a shower one hour before his dental appointment. He was just sitting in his chair, not watching TV, not listening to the radio, and not even drinking his coffee. Absolutely nothing! I asked if he was going to the dentist, and he said, "Yes." It was as if he was sleeping with his eyes open, deep in thought!

In August, we had the appointment with our family doctor about Rick's memory. He passed his Alzheimer's test, and the doctor didn't feel Rick's problem was anything physical. However, he suspected there might be some arterial disease in the brain's vessels and/or that Rick was suffering from depression. He also suggested that Rick probably hadn't learned communication skills very well because, as a boss giving orders, his employees just did as they were told. The doctor followed up with lab work and ordered an MRI of the brain.

The MRI results showed age-related mild to moderate hardening of the arteries.

Apparently, it wasn't severe enough to label his memory loss as dementia. So, what were we dealing with? We couldn't deny that there were serious issues with his memory, but there was no definite diagnosis.

It had been a stressful time at our house, but a visit from my niece Debbie from California gave us a much-needed break. We took a drive up to Zion with Rick at the wheel. After we entered the tunnel and needed to turn the headlights on, he couldn't find the switch. He continued to drive with one hand on the wheel and the other hand fumbling at the dashboard as the tunnel got darker and darker. Debbie and I almost went into panic mode, but our Angels kept us safe as we made it through the tunnel in the dark before finally seeing daylight.

Luckily, we arrived back in town and drove past the Masonic Lodge to show Debbie. I told Rick I wanted to go home via River Road, but he was completely turned around as to which direction to go. By this time of day, he was getting tired and not at his best. It's called "Sundowners."

The following day, I had been out shopping and was locked out of the house when I returned. The door leading from the garage into the house was usually unlocked, but the deadbolt was locked for the second time in recent days, and I didn't have a key for that lock. After he came to let me in, I asked why he was locking the door, but he had no reason.

***

Labor Day weekend in 2012 started off with Rick going over to Camping World to pick up the trailer after having some work done on the air conditioner. He climbed on top of the trailer to inspect the A/C but missed a couple of steps on the ladder coming back down, falling four to five feet onto the asphalt and landing on his back! Despite being in a lot of pain, he managed to drive home without the trailer, as the work had not been completed as he had been told.

Rick went to the ER, where X-rays showed contusions of the rib cage but no broken bones. However, over time, his lower back began to hurt more, and his left leg became increasingly painful. Over the following months, he made many visits to the chiropractor, receiving adjustments, decompression, and laser treatments. He was also scheduled for an MRI of his back. The results showed three bulging discs and a large area of arthritis. Chiropractic treatments continued until he was referred to a pain management doctor, who administered four epidural injections spread out over a period of time. Unfortunately, these were unsuccessful, and his leg pain continued to worsen. In early December, Rick found himself back in the ER after driving home from California with severe leg pain. They checked for blood clots but found none.

***

A new year had begun, and it felt good to close out the old one, hoping for a fresh start with 2013—if that was even possible! Rick was still trying to manage simple chores, but sometimes, he even lost track of what day it was. He'd forget things like putting out the trash barrels and many days, he seemed very childlike. Our relationship had gradually shifted to one that felt more like that of a parent and child.

Like a teacher, I began giving him assignments because he didn't seem to notice when things needed to be done. I told him his desk needed dusting, so he did it. Then I mentioned the garage needed attention—trash needed to be thrown out, items put away that he'd dragged out but hadn't put away, and RV supplies sorted for reuse, disposal, or sale. He did as I asked.

While he was in the garage, I brought out a timer and told him to come in for lunch when he heard the bell. He was always ready to eat, so he came in quickly when it rang. While he ate, I placed some mail next to him to read, but I noticed later that he had just tossed it aside when he was finished. During this time, I was busy clearing the dishes, loading the dishwasher, wiping the counters, cleaning the sinks and microwave, and taking out the trash.

When I was done, I looked up to find him standing beside his chair, completely engrossed in a movie we were watching. He hadn't even offered to help. I asked if he wanted the mail, and he simply said, "No." He could have thrown it away himself but left it for me instead. Again, I was supposed to read his mind!

Not long ago, he asked if I wanted a Dr. Pepper or Root Beer from the garage refrigerator. I said, "Dr. Pepper." But I ended up with a Root Beer—he thought that's what I'd said! No, it wasn't!

We had a new ice cream scoop that was supposed to be hand-washed. I told him before we ever used it that it shouldn't go into the dishwasher, but I had to remind him again when I retrieved it just before it went into the wash. About a month later, I was unloading the dishwasher and found the scoop. I mentioned to Rick that it had somehow ended up with the dirty dishes, and he said, "I know; it was down in the silverware compartment!" Yes, he admitted he knew it was there but didn't realize that *that* was the scoop I meant!

The faucet in the laundry room was leaking, and Rick thought he could easily fix it. Unlike the old days when a quick 1-2-3 fix at home was standard, it turned into 1-2-3 trips to the hardware store. First, he went to buy gaskets, but they didn't stop the leak. He went back to the store and came home with a new faucet, but it was brass instead of chrome. He grew frustrated with himself as things took much longer than they used to. But he had never been a quitter before dementia set in, so he kept pushing on until the job was done.

After he finished fixing the faucet, I started doing laundry but ended up with water all over the floor. Thankfully, he managed to tighten the hoses and stopped that leak!

The next day, I asked if he knew the shower handle was loose, but he had no idea. He didn't seem to notice anything until I pointed it out, even though he'd used the shower earlier. He tightened the handle and asked if I thought it was better. "Of course, it's better, thank you!" I replied.

His eyesight was getting worse, but he kept quiet about it, not wanting others, including me, to know how bad it had become. One example was when he cut his toenails too short, causing one to bleed. He put Mercurochrome and a band-aid on the big toe. The next morning, he said it was better but still sore. I noticed the toe looked redder than the medicine would have caused, so I suggested he put Aloe Vera on instead. He repeatedly asked if I thought the Aloe would be better, and I replied, somewhat impatiently, "I already told you!"

We had reached a point where Rick still believed he was capable of handling many tasks he used to do, but I wasn't so sure anymore. I found myself constantly "on the fence," unsure whether he was capable or not of doing so many things. We spent many days struggling to pretend that everything was normal, even though deep down, both of us knew our lives weren't improving. It felt like I was caught between a rock and a hard spot, wanting life to be as normal as it once was but unsure when to speak up, keep quiet, ignore the mistakes, or quietly fix them and move on.

One day, he took on the task of talking to a new agent over the phone about our auto and homeowners insurance. At that time, many people still weren't aware of the struggles Rick was facing. Fortunately, the agent conducted business as usual, and luckily, this turned out to be one of Rick's successful ventures. These were the kinds of tasks he had always handled for us in the past, but now, entrusting him with such responsibilities felt like a gamble.

That year was one of the toughest, watching Rick go through good days, bad days, moments of sound judgment, and lapses in judgment. Just when I'd think, "*He's back*," something would happen to erase my confidence all over again.

We took Kurly (KQ for short) to the vet for a checkup when he was sick. The assistant asked what his vomit had looked like. For example, was it white and foamy? Rick quickly answered, "Yes," but I had to correct him, saying, "No!" He had no idea what it looked like but wanted to appear as though he was on top of things, even though he hadn't seen it. After the appointment, with our fur baby ready to go home, sitting between us in the car, Rick started the engine and tried to exit the parking lot—only to realize he hadn't released the brake!

One evening, Rick took KQ outside to go potty and then brought him back into the kitchen. He shut the gate and left the dog in the dark room. Of course, the barking started—not from me, but from the dog! I went into the kitchen and rescued KQ. I couldn't help but wonder what had been going through Rick's mind to leave the dog in a dark room when we were just in the next room watching TV. That wasn't something he had ever done before.

Another time, he was trying to ask me a question, but his words came out completely garbled. I told him to start over, and he replied, "If I knew what I wanted to say, I'd say it!" He tried again, and I managed to guess what he was trying to say, so I finished the question for him.

A couple of days later, I was applying Bona to our wooden floors when I had to stop and leave for a doctor's appointment. Rick offered to continue the job while I was gone, so I explained what I had already done and what still needed to be finished. However, as I was leaving, I noticed he was working on the section I had already completed. We exchanged a few words, and he admitted that he hadn't understood what I had told him.

It was becoming increasingly apparent that Rick wasn't noticing things he used to, like when he needed a haircut. He had been overdue for one for over a week, so I decided to see how long it would take for him to bring it up. I couldn't keep quiet any longer and finally mentioned it one evening. Then he asked if I could give him a haircut the next morning!

I also asked him to redline his medication list so I could update it in my Excel program. He was more engrossed in a TV show than in focusing on the list. When he finally handed it back to me, I noticed he had crossed out a medication he had just recently started. I pointed out that it shouldn't be removed, but he insisted he hadn't taken that medication in a long time. This made me start wondering if he should no longer be in charge of his meds. However, bringing up the possibility that he was no longer capable of managing them was a delicate subject.

The previous week, I had asked him how many test strips he had left to check his blood sugar, but he never gave me a straight answer. I went ahead and ordered more, then asked him what his sugar numbers had been lately. He admitted he didn't know because he had run out of test strips!

One day, he climbed a ladder to change a light bulb and suddenly experienced extreme fatigue and weakness while still on the ladder. When I took his blood pressure after he came down, it was alarmingly low—68/49. After calling the cardiology office, they advised me to take him to the ER, where they did lab work and an EKG. The new diagnosis, added to his growing list of medical issues, was congestive heart failure (CHF), likely due to the dose of blood pressure medication he was taking, which also explained the swelling in his feet. His cardiologist immediately reduced the dosage, and his symptoms improved.

When our Social Security 1099s arrived, Rick tried to read his but got stuck on the phrase "paid by check or direct deposit." He asked, "What is this?" I explained, "It's the money we receive from them." His response was, "From who?"

I spent hours compiling medical expenses to prepare our taxes and handed Rick a three-page recap of the expenses to review. He just stared at the top page, seemingly uninterested or unable to understand. I told him he needed to look at the next two pages to see the full results, but at that moment, I realized it would be the last time I'd ask him to review anything related to taxes or finances. He simply wasn't there anymore.

Rick's friend Bob had recently received a new pacemaker, and Rick offered to take him to a doctor's appointment after Bob had fallen twice. When Rick returned home, he told me everything checked out OK, but he mentioned that Bob was really losing it and should be in an Assisted Living Facility. A few days later, Rick was recounting Bob's fall to someone else, mentioning that Bob had banged up his head, broken his glasses, and gotten a black eye. He had never told me any of those details before, so I was left wondering—did he make it up, or did he just forget to tell me?

Rick bought two cellophane-wrapped packs of wood for the fireplace, which was great, but he placed them on the stack of wood inside the house instead of outside on the patio. Now, I was left with the choice of either taking them outside and removing the packaging myself or asking him to do it.

It was time to sell the Ford F-150 and trailer we owned—a sad decision but a necessary one since traveling was no longer in the cards for us. Fortunately, someone at an RV dealership wanted to buy the truck for himself and had a buyer lined up for the trailer, making it a win-win sale. However, when Rick took a call from the buyer regarding checks and titles, he struggled to relay the message to me later, unable to remember the details.

One morning, he asked me, "How did you sleep last night?" I replied, "OK." He then said he'd heard me rattling around all night. Surprised, I responded, "No, you didn't! I only got up once early this morning; otherwise, I was sleeping most of the night!"

His reply? "Well, then, it must have all been in my head!"

On another occasion, Rick put a load of laundry in the wash before leaving for a meeting and asked me to put it in the dryer when it was done. I thought, "*What's going on? He NEVER does laundry!*" He explained that he was washing his whites because he was out. When I asked if he had included my whites as well (we kept them in separate hampers), he said he didn't know I needed any washed. It was doubtful he was truly out of underwear, but that's just how his mind was working that day.

Then there was the time he tossed a shirt into the washing machine after I had already started a load and left the room. When I discovered his orange shirt mixed in with the whites, I was livid. His only apology was that he thought I was washing colored clothes. I couldn't help but wonder, *"What made him think that?"* Oh, if only I could keep up with him!

My patience was wearing thin, and my frustration was growing. It was time for another heart-to-heart talk, with a list of concerns that kept getting longer. First, he told me forty minutes before we were supposed to leave for his doctor's appointment that KQ was all ready, but he hadn't taken him out for a potty break or secured him in the kitchen as usual. Second, he just sat and watched TV until it was finally time to leave. Third, he never brought the trash barrel in from the curb after it had been emptied. Fourth, the bird feeder had been empty for at least five days. Fifth, the hummingbird feeder had gone dry the day before. Sixth, the bird bath was also dry. Seventh, he went to physical therapy and came home only to sit around, playing musical chairs, while I worked myself to the point of no return! I felt more like a mother than a wife. Eighth, he never volunteered to help or noticed anything that needed to be done anymore. He was in his own little world while everything was done for him. And if he did do something, I felt I had better check to see what he had done.

I suggested that he join me in the garage to help gather items for another upcoming yard sale. He went out and just stood around, watching me. After picking up a few things and inspecting them, he did manage to add a few items to the sale pile. But when I asked him about a couple of items from his collection, he admitted he didn't even know what they were.

Through the years, we had quite a few successful yard sales. Everything was always clean and priced, with repeat customers waiting outside by seven a.m. before the sale even started. In the early days, Rick was an excellent teammate during those yard sales, and it was a fun adventure for both of us. But those days were behind us; he was no longer the reliable helper I could once depend on.

I went into the house for a few minutes and, upon returning to the garage, saw him jump when he heard me come back in. I had already noticed him standing there, staring at the table, when I opened the door, but he seemed to feel the need to offer an explanation, starting to say he was just... Many times, he would tell me he was doing "something" when, in reality, I would still find him simply staring into space, doing nothing.

After our little heart-to-heart talk before the yard sale, Rick actually became more active afterward, making up for lost time. He filled the bird feeder and bird bath, put away the tables we had used, and returned unsold items to the shed. Then, he even took the car for an oil change. It was a big accomplishment for him in one day and a huge help to me.

When Rick started taking Gabapentin for pain, he was given specific instructions on how to gradually increase the dosage. I thought he understood the instructions, as he had indicated to the doctor, so I continued to let him manage his own daily medications. However, when I checked with him a few days later, I was horrified by how he recounted the doctor's instructions. His only response was, "At least I'm still alive."

His feet had been hurting more, especially on the tops and all of his toes, and he suspected the Gabapentin was causing his feet to swell. He left a message for the doctor because he thought he needed a higher dose. I was trying to be more understanding, more patient, more helpful, more supportive—doing more and more for him. It felt like my plate was overflowing!

I had a big box to mail at the post office, so Rick drove me there. As we entered the roundabout, he pulled right in front of another car and then missed the entrance to the parking lot, heading instead toward the outside mail drop. When I told him I needed to go inside, he made a U-turn and finally entered the parking lot. We made it without a dent or a scratch!

In March, a neurologist came on board and gave Rick a complete evaluation. She reviewed the MRI results of his back from last November and confirmed that he had spinal deterioration as well as stenosis caused by arthritis. She also performed an EMG with a nerve stimulation test, revealing severe nerve damage in his left leg that was caused by his fall off of the RV ladder. Her office contacted the Barrow Neurological Institute in Chandler, AZ, to get him help sooner than what was available in Utah. They also canceled the injections Rick had been receiving in his back and sent his records to Barrow, emphasizing that his condition had progressed and was deteriorating rapidly.

We made two trips to Barrow in April to meet with a neurosurgeon. During the first trip, the surgeon conducted an extensive evaluation, studied Rick's MRI, and determined that surgery was indeed necessary to relieve the severe pain. The MRI also revealed a second area that could cause future problems involving his arms, so we agreed to address both areas during the same surgery. Rick was scheduled for immediate surgery, but first, he needed approval from his cardiologist in St. George. Unfortunately, that approval was denied, so we headed home to schedule an appointment with that doctor.

After receiving approval from the cardiologist, Rick's surgery was rescheduled for April 29th. We made another trip to Chandler and stayed in Scottsdale at a timeshare we owned. Rick's surgery went well; he underwent a left L5-S1 Micro-lumbar Discectomy (MLD) with the removal of calcification (arthritis) and a T11-12 Laminectomy to address nerve root decompression.

The drive home after his discharge from the hospital was quite an experience. We had to stop every hour so Rick could walk for ten minutes with his walker to prevent blood clots. After weeks of physical therapy in St. George, he recovered, but he was never quite one hundred percent again.

I continued driving more often after his surgery. I told Rick that I felt all the medications he was taking were impairing his judgment, and I no longer felt comfortable riding with him. He didn't resist and seemed content to be a passenger at that time.

Following his physical therapy, I suggested Rick start doing some light tasks outside, like filling the birdbath and feeding the birds again. It wasn't heavy work, but his legs and feet continued to ache whenever he did anything. One day, I thought some ice might help, and he asked if we had any. Of course, we had ice packs in the freezer, but his subtle hint was for me to get one for him. After all, I had been waiting on him throughout his recovery. I would have preferred if he had just asked for the ice directly, but I had to accept that our thoughts didn't always align. Despite this, I continued to do more for him, as his needs seemed to increase rather than decrease.

The less Rick did and the more I took on, the more time he spent in front of the TV or sitting at the computer. Sometimes, when I was in the kitchen preparing a meal, he would come in and just stand there, watching me. His idea of helping might be placing two napkins on the table, and with that, his job was done. One time, after putting the napkins down, he sat on his stool and then asked me to get him a fork!

During this period, it became noticeable that Rick had started dragging his feet when he walked. He also mentioned feeling "yucky" on many days, which was likely due to all the medications, but we couldn't be sure. Keeping track of his medications became a full-time job, as every visit to a different doctor often resulted in a new prescription or a change in his regimen. This put extra pressure on his primary physician, who specialized in Internal Medicine.

I maintained an up-to-date database on the computer, tracking all of Rick's prescriptions, supplements, and medical history, always keeping a current copy in our wallets to ensure we had it on hand whenever needed.

In April 2013, our primary doctor started Rick on Lantus Insulin for his diabetes, discontinuing Metformin and Glipizide since those pills seemed to upset his stomach. Rick was able to give himself the insulin shots without any help, and he still managed to keep track of his daily pills—or so I thought. He had convinced me that he was still capable of handling them.

So, since he was still in charge of his daily pills after I had filled his weekly pill box, I assumed he would adjust his weekly box whenever a doctor changed a prescription during that week. However, on one occasion, he was supposed to stop his blood thinner for three days but forgot to remove those pills from his box. I suggested that I start managing all his pills, as it seemed to be getting more challenging for him, but he disagreed and insisted he could still do it himself.

Eventually, I realized he was struggling with giving himself the insulin shots as well. Sometimes, the needle would bend as he pulled it out, or maybe it bent when he pushed it in, and I worried that a piece could break off. Other times, he wasn't sure the insulin had been injected properly, so he would ask me to check, and I'd find that the insulin had sometimes run down the outside instead of going in.

Managing medications is a significant responsibility for any caregiver. Deciding when to take over or continue letting the patient manage their own medications is an incredibly difficult decision. It's far better to take on those responsibilities before something goes wrong—sooner rather than later. Every situation is different, so there's no one-size-fits-all advice I can give. In our case,

I should have taken over those duties much sooner than I did. Patients, especially those with dementia, often insist they are perfectly capable of giving their own shots, distributing their pills, and taking them as prescribed. But more often than not, they need your help.

CHAPTER 03 | Slowly Drifting

When it came time for Rick to renew his driver's license, he needed to fill out an application. He didn't bring any of the required documents, like a birth certificate or proof of residency. They gave him a number, and we waited for what felt like an eternity to hear his number be called over the loudspeaker. After a long wait, Rick turned to me and asked if I thought he should go up and inquire. I said, "Yes," but he just sat there. A little later, he asked me again, and again I said, "Yes!" Finally, he got up and asked someone behind the counter if they had called his number, and they told him they had. So, he was given a new number, and the wait began all over again.

Throughout this experience, and many others, I found myself wondering whether Rick was still capable of handling routine tasks or if I should have stepped up to the plate. I didn't want to make him feel inadequate and hoped he could still manage some things on his own. As I mentioned before, some days, I felt like a teacher watching over his shoulder to see if he was doing his assignments correctly. Other days, I felt like a mother, quietly fixing things behind him.

As much as I thought I was helping, I gradually realized there were other areas where he really needed assistance. The tasks he had handled for so many years were things I just assumed he could still do. It hadn't always occurred to me that certain things were being neglected and that he needed more support. As the saying goes, "You don't know what you don't know."

One day, I called him from the store and asked if he could preheat the oven to 400 degrees because I was bringing home a pizza. When I got home, the oven was still preheating. I asked, "You didn't turn the oven on when I called, did you?" He said he had, but didn't remember to press the "start" button until he went back into the kitchen later.

All the doctor appointments became so routine that, most days, they just felt like another place to go. During one visit to the chiropractor, Rick was reliving the days when we first knew each other at work. We had known each other for about five years before we started dating and were married less than a year after that first date. He told the doctor we had dated for five years, and I stood behind him, rolling my eyes!

The neurologist was desperately trying to find new medications to relieve Rick's pain. He was told he had a cyst on his right kidney, based on a new CAT scan, but no treatment was advised. She also said he didn't have Parkinson's disease, but less than three months later, she suggested that his speech issues and falls might be symptoms pointing in that direction. She also believed that the pain in his feet was due to muscles and tendons, not neuropathy, so she recommended topical creams and patches. Those didn't work either!

I have some old family paintings that I inherited from my grandmother, and I called someone in California to see about getting them appraised. When I showed them to Rick, he suddenly raised his voice, interrupted me, and shouted, "I PAINTED THAT PICTURE FOR A GROUP OF WOMEN!" I explained who actually painted the pictures, but he insisted, "I DON'T KNOW WHO THAT PERSON IS!" Clearly, that conversation wasn't going anywhere.

This pattern repeated itself time and again—I would try to initiate a meaningful conversation, only to be met with silence. For example, one day, I shared something new with him, but he just looked at me with no emotion and said nothing. The next night, there was absolutely no conversation at dinner, except for one comment that was a repeat of what he had said at lunchtime about liking the frosting on the cake. So, sometimes, I chose not to say anything when I felt it was going to be a one-way street. If I didn't start a conversation, there simply wasn't one. Occasionally, I would tell him something, and he would just nod his head "yes," as if agreeing with me. Then I'd find out later that he didn't even know what I had said if I may have asked a related question and needed an answer. Silence. I often had to remind him that I had just asked him a question!

We went to Denny's for dinner one night. Our check was $17.12, and I gave him $20.12 to pay. There were lots of people waiting to pay at the register, but he walked right up to the counter and put his money down. I had to remind him that all those people were waiting ahead of us. When it was finally his turn, he placed the check and money on the counter and walked away. Again, I had to tell him to go back and get the change. We had reached the point where he carried less and less money in his wallet because he couldn't tell one denomination from another and seemed too careless with it. He argued at first, insisting he should have at least $100 in his wallet, but sometimes the caregiver needs to put their foot down. I started giving him more bills but less money, like four $5 bills or twenty $1 bills.

Every day was a surprise. He had pain in his big toe, so I made an appointment with the foot doctor for two o'clock. I gave him all the information at the breakfast table in writing. At one-fifty, I found him sitting at his computer and told him he'd better get going. "Oh, I thought it was at two-thirty! Who am I going to see?" At that point, he was still driving and wanted me to believe he could keep track of time, and I wanted to believe it, too. He was changing, and that meant I had to change as well. We were both becoming strangers to each other.

The house phone rang, and I yelled from the other room not to answer it because it was a solicitor. I saw the green light go on, meaning he had picked up the phone. He claimed he was on his cell phone and didn't answer the house phone, but I had seen that green light. Figure that one out!

We went to the Elks Lodge for dinner on a "steak" night, and Rick pulled out his membership card to enter. After we were inside, a lady from the lobby came in looking for Rick with a handful of cards that had fallen out of his wallet! Another time, he forgot his cap when we left, and someone had to come outside to flag us down as we were about to drive away. Thank goodness, those Elks are a bunch of honest people!

It was becoming noticeable that using a napkin at the table was a thing of the past. It became somewhat embarrassing when he would continue eating with food on his face. Reminding him to use his napkin became routine, especially when others were around.

He was back to driving once his back surgery had healed, but not very well, in my opinion. I found myself backseat driving more and more to help us get from point A to point B as safely as possible. One trip to the local post office proved my point. We were too late for that day's pickup, so we headed to another post office in a neighboring city. He made a wrong turn and ended up in a shopping center parking lot. With a deadline to meet at the next post office, we were running out of time. I told him to forget the mail, and, well, let's just say his response was less than pleasant.

Sometimes, it took everything I had to keep my cool. There were days when I felt like I didn't know this man anymore or what might come out of his mouth next. For instance, I walked into his room while he was on the computer, just to tell him about a phone call I had received. I noticed he was looking at Class B RVs, but he quickly exited the screen when he saw me. Later on, I mentioned that I had seen him looking at RVs, and he told me with a straight face that he was researching the procedure for an EMG! Yellow flag, or red flag? My caution flags had started going up shortly after we were married, unfortunately. It's incredibly disappointing to be so certain you've seen or heard something you wished you hadn't. Through the years, I would let each incident go and try to enjoy the next magical moment we could experience together.

Not long after, Rick actually volunteered to wash some windows and had just gone outside as I was returning from an appointment. It turned out there was a reason for his sudden enthusiasm—he admitted that he had accidentally sprayed the windows with Miracle-Gro weeks earlier while doing yard work, and I thought they were just dirty! He had done a good job with the yard, but the windows had suffered for it.

Another incident occurred on Blackridge Drive when he was driving down the hill at 45 mph, headed straight for the curb! I initially touched his arm and yelled to get his attention. When he barely missed the curb, I shouted, "What in the H-E-Q-Q were you doing?" No answer.

By this time, Rick was getting increasingly discouraged and discussed his frustrations with our primary physician. His memory was fading in and out, his legs were getting weaker, his balance was worsening, and his falls were unpredictable. He spent many days just not feeling well, suffering from head congestion or an upset stomach. Some days, he wasn't even motivated to get dressed or do the few chores he was still able to manage. He mentioned that he was getting tired of all the pain.

Rick had struggled with bouts of depression

his entire life, as he openly admitted to the doctor, so all these medical issues were an overwhelming burden. He reached a point where he didn't have much to say to me anymore, yet he would talk and talk to someone else if they were around. Sometimes, he even talked to our dog more than he talked to me! He might occasionally comment on something I had said, but often, it was just a one-word response or a vague reply that could apply to anything. I wondered if he was even listening to me.

After that discussion with the doctor, I realized I was dealing with more than just his medical issues. Life, in general, is not easy; but you have to make an effort, keep pushing, don't give up, try again, admit your weaknesses, get help, communicate, and pray! Trying to help someone with medical issues is a lot of work, but adding depression to the mix is a whole other challenge. Now, I understood much more than I had before.

Our friend from California stopped by to see us on his way to Wyoming, so we decided to take him to the Golden Corral for lunch. I made sure Rick had enough cash on him to pay. When we got to the cashier, I was first in line, Rick was second and took out two $20 bills to pay, and our guest was behind him. Our tall friend said something to him, and Rick said, "OK," and put his money away. I shot Rick a dirty look, and he glared back, saying, "What? You want me to pay?" That was one of my most embarrassing moments.

When our friend left the next morning, I sent him off with a goody bag for the road. I had made cranberry salad and put some in a used butter container, telling him what it was, with Rick sitting right there, listening. Later that night at dinner, Rick said it was nice of me to have given our friend some butter to take with him, which led to another frustrating conversation. Really? When our friend arrived in Wyoming, he called and mentioned how windy it was there. The phone was on speaker so Rick could listen too. Later during dinner, Rick told me it was very windy in Wyoming, as if it was new information.

A fire was raging in California near where we used to live and where two of our grandchildren lived. After hearing the news broadcast, I went into the other room and told Rick what I had just heard. Fifteen minutes later, he came into the kitchen and said he missed the news about the fire and asked, "Where did you say it was?" A couple of days later, there was another update on the fire, and Rick commented while watching it on TV that this was the first he had heard about it!

Here's another example of a typical conversation about his medication: He asked me if I had any Tylenol. I grabbed the bottle from my bathroom and gave him two pills. Then I checked his bathroom cupboard and found no Tylenol, but I did find his bottle of pain pills with only six pills left. He had told the neurologist he was trying to wean off the pain pills and had about seven left. If he was in pain, why didn't he take one of those pills? I then asked if he had already taken the Tylenol, and he said, "No." I asked for the two pills back and told him to take a pain pill instead. Then he said he had already taken one Tylenol and was saving the other one for after dinner.

Mixed messages are what many conversations led to those days. I could almost count on "no," meaning "yes," and "yes," meaning "no." He confused me so much that I didn't know what to believe half the time, but I couldn't afford to guess!

It got to the point where Rick was frequently

knocking over beverage glasses at the table, and I asked him if he thought his eyesight might be worsening. He blamed his clumsiness on the side effects of Gabapentin. If I had blamed the medicine, he probably would have blamed his eyesight! His logic didn't make much sense to me most of the time, and he no longer seemed like the smartest man I knew. It was so hard watching him slowly drift away from the vibrant, full-of-life person he was when I married him. It felt like he was retreating into a cocoon within his own world. As the months turned into years, I had to face the realization that our better days were behind us. The future was a mystery, and I knew I would need to rely on my faith to get through whatever my tomorrows would bring.

He had an appointment with a new ophthalmologist in June for a glaucoma and cataract evaluation. During the initial visit, the doctor said glaucoma was "iffy" at that point, but cataract surgeries were highly recommended. The pressure in his left eye was consistently above the normal range, so the plan was to insert a stent in that eye during the cataract surgery to help keep the pressure down. There was a history of high pressure in the left eye, as recorded at each retina appointment.

Rick was given instructions for various eye drops to be used before and after the surgeries. While I took notes, Rick indicated that he understood exactly what he was supposed to do. With all the prescriptions filled and carefully set out with a schedule to mark off the days and times, it seemed like everything was under control.

One particular eye drop was for the left eye to be applied twice a day. I believed he was following the directions until one morning, I noticed his right eye looked watery when he entered the kitchen for breakfast. When I asked about it, he said he had just put the eye drops in—but they were in the wrong eye! Those drops were supposed to go into his left eye in preparation for the stent insertion during surgery.

At his next pre-op visit, the doctor asked if he had put the drops in his left eye that morning. Rick responded that he hadn't used the drops since his injection from the retina specialist the week before. The doctor had planned to check his eye pressure after he had been using the drops, but by that time, no one knew what

Rick had actually been doing. Fortunately, his cataract surgery went well, and the stent in his left eye kept the pressure down within the normal range.

Another eye doctor was consulted to evaluate whether his eyelids were contributing to his vision problems, as his ophthalmologist suspected. After a thorough evaluation and visual field testing of his upper vision, it was confirmed that eyelid surgery would be beneficial.

That surgery was completed in October, four months after his initial exam. However, his blood pressure soared to 222/136 during the procedure, and they had to quickly administer medication to bring it down. By the time he was released to go home, the numbers had dropped to 136/87.

When they escorted him into the lobby, I was shocked by the appearance of his right eye. It had a wide-open stare, looking off to the right, while the left eye looked natural and focused straight ahead. In time, his eyes relaxed and looked more normal, but it always seemed like his right eye had been overdone. As the years passed, his eyelids gradually returned to their original appearance, as if he had never had any eyelid surgery at all.

Post-op visits became routine, and managing his eye medication schedule became a full-time job. Rick was always a good patient, willing to try anything that might make him better. But "better" always seemed just out of reach for him.

We had an appointment with the neurologist in July. In desperation, I slipped her a note asking for help with Rick's memory issues, which he didn't think were a problem on that particular day. Our communication was nearly nonexistent most days; he just didn't comprehend what I was saying and often came back with the most bewildering answers!

One day, after Rick had left for physical therapy, I noticed a smudge on the shower door handle. As I went over to clean it, I discovered the handle was broken! It had been replaced about two years before, so there was no reason for it to be broken. Rick never mentioned it, even though he must have noticed when he took his shower. Ignoring an issue wasn't new for him; I had learned years ago that this was part of his personality. To ignore something meant he didn't have to deal with it.

Two days after driving to physical therapy, he couldn't find his car keys but eventually found them in his coin jar, where he had put them! He had also stopped doing his physical therapy exercises at home, although he still kept his appointments. When I asked if he had lost interest in PT, he simply said, "No, I just haven't been doing it."

He fell in August when his legs gave out on him while he was out in the yard. He ended up in a sitting position, not once but twice. He managed to get to the porch and sit down until he could retrieve his walker from the garage. Although he could still walk without a cane or walker, it was highly discouraged. He just didn't want to give up his independence and was determined to do things on his own.

There was another fall in September—this time, he climbed a ladder in the living room. You might wonder what in the heck he was doing on a ladder at that point, but he still believed he could do whatever he wanted. I knew just how far to push his buttons and when to stop. When I couldn't be in charge, someone higher up would have to take over.

Thankfully, he wasn't hurt when he pulled the

ladder down with him as he hit the carpet. He said he caught his foot on something while trying to slide it over on the step. I never quite understood his explanation, but it was yet another fall to add to the list.

In October, he fell backward in the house while stooping over but wasn't hurt this time either. The following day, he was carrying our dog, KQ, into the house when he tripped on the patio step and fell into the screen door. This time, he fell on his right hip, cut one finger, and scraped both arms.

Rick continued to experience a lot of nausea from all the medications he was either starting, increasing, or decreasing. He had a gallbladder function test in October that revealed it didn't completely empty, but it wasn't serious enough to treat at that point.

There were two more falls in November. One was at our local Honda dealer, where he missed a step in the parking lot, fell onto one knee, and cut his hand in two places. The other fall happened when he stumbled backward while the two of us were carrying a bike rack from the backyard to the driveway. He fell on his left hip and ended up bruised and sore.

He fell twice in December. The first time, he stumbled over a decorative Christmas sleigh on the family room's hardwood floor but, fortunately, wasn't hurt.

The second fall occurred when his sleeve caught on a piece of metal hinge from the garage door, which caused him to fall into a sitting position. One arm had four long, deep gouges above and below the elbow that bled profusely. This fall sent us to the ER, where he received a tetanus shot, and they scrubbed and wrapped the wounds. There was nothing to stitch. The wounds continued to ooze for the next ten days, and blood-soaked bandages had to be changed often. Because there were no witnesses, I tried to re-enact his version of how the accident happened, but I could never quite piece the puzzle together.

A Christmas package arrived from one of his daughters, wrapped in parcel paper. Rick proceeded to unwrap the package and saw that the box said it contained a one-at-a-time-cup coffee maker. He studied the box, read each side, left it on the floor, and exited the room! When I noticed the box was still on the floor, sealed with packing tape, I opened it and found wrapped presents and pictures inside, which I then showed to Rick. Later that day, while we were eating at a restaurant, the subject of the box came up. Rick said, "I need to open that box and figure out that coffee pot!"

***

The following year was 2014, and it started just like 2013 had ended, but with even more unpredictables! Our calendar was full of cardiology, audiology, neurology, ophthalmology, podiatry, retina, ENT, internist, physical therapy, dental, Insta Care, and ER visits. It seemed as though every doctor referred him to another!

However, I must start out on the humorous side so as not to give the impression every day was one negative after another, even if some humor resulted from a stupid mistake! As I've mentioned before, we tried to start each day as normal as one could be. So, here is the story about meatballs!

We had gone shopping at Costco the day before and bought a large package of frozen meatballs. When we got home, I asked him to put all the frozen groceries in the garage freezer, including the meatballs. Assuming I could depend on him to do something that simple, I went inside and finished up in the kitchen. Just to make sure, because I was never sure, I asked if he had put everything in the freezer, and he answered, "Yes"! The next day, I found the package of meatballs in the refrigerator completely thawed out! Oh my gosh, I didn't know whether to be mad or glad that I had discovered them that soon. So, I threw them in the freezer in hopes it wasn't too late, and apparently, they hadn't spoiled, or I wouldn't be here to tell about the meatball story!

January wasn't without incident when he misjudged a sharp corner of the wall bed in our guest room. He fell to the floor and said his legs didn't feel strong. The neurologist did an arterial ultrasound on his legs a few days later that turned out normal! He started Cinamet on a trial basis since all his falls, speech, as well as his head hanging down when he walked, were classic symptoms of Parkinson's. This diagnosis was contrary to her medical opinion three months prior, but as it turned out, she was correct this time.

He continued to drive and chauffeured me to an appointment one day in February. When we got back to the car, he had lost his car keys, but fortunately, someone had turned them into the front desk when he went back inside to look for them! He also hoped to eat lunch anytime we were out for appointments, and that day was no exception. Once we entered Olive Garden, he couldn't find his glasses until I told him he was wearing them!

After lunch, he was driving down Main Street and didn't see a car stopped at a crosswalk. If I hadn't been paying attention and yelled to stop, he would have plowed right into the back of that car at maybe 30-35 mph. I asked, "What were you looking at?" He said nonchalantly, "Nothing!" I think that should have been his last day of driving, but a few days later, we had a conversation, and he actually told me quite seriously that he was a better driver than I was!

Two more falls happened in February. The first one occurred in the backyard, where he fell into the rocks but shouldn't have been trying to walk over them in the first place. He hit his right shoulder, right hip, and the left side of his chest. Trying to picture that fall and hurting both sides may be difficult, but the next day, he was very sore in those areas. Physical therapy was recommended for his balance a few days later, so PT started again. The second fall happened on the front porch about ten days later. Fortunately, he didn't fall hard enough to cause any damage.

One thing he got credit for was to always try and protect his head during those falls!

It was the middle of February when I had been in the kitchen a good two hours preparing our Sunday meal consisting of salmon loaf, SF Jello, SF cranberry Jello salad, broccoli-cheese rice, a green salad, and plans to put an angel-food cake in the oven as soon as we finished dinner. Rick was at the sink putting dishes in the dishwasher while I was fixing the cake to go into the oven.

Once in the oven, I proceeded to wash the countertops not paying attention to Rick. He opened the oven to put the broiler pan inside and informed me I already had a cake in the oven, all the time holding the oven door open! I yelled, "My cake! Shut the door, or the cake will fall!" What's more, the broiler pan belonged in the drawer underneath the oven.

The following day, I reminded him that he had a chiropractic appointment at twelve-thirty the next day and PT right after at one forty-five. He understood that his two appointments were both PT, and he was argumentive, knowing too much, too soon! Telling him that far in advance was very confusing, and I was beginning to realize that I shouldn't tell him anything the day before.

In March, he fell off the step going outside to the patio and ended up with a bloody knee and twisted ankle. Three days later, he caught his foot on the doggy gate as he tried stepping over it instead of opening the gate and walking through. He fell on the tile floor, hitting his left shoulder and hip. By that evening, he was hurting again!

I mentioned that night that it must be getting old, falling so much, and I had mentioned throughout the day that he might need to use his walker more often to prevent falls. He thought there must be something more that was causing him to fall besides just plain clumsiness, and I explained that that was what the neurologist was trying to figure out. He actually had no clue or memory of anything she had told him, and from the tone of his voice, I knew he really had no idea what was wrong, when it started, or why he fell off the RV ladder. He had made a comment one time that he couldn't figure out why he missed those steps climbing off the RV roof.

He said he finally figured out the reason why he was falling so much. It was his glasses, so he quit wearing them! The glasses were only three months old, and he was falling before that.

During that same week, he woke up one morning and opened the sliding glass door before shutting off the security alarm. When we left to take the dog to the groomer, he couldn't find his cane but finally did. As he was backing out of the driveway, he headed straight for the mailbox! I spoke up, and he said with a flippant attitude that he knew how to drive. Before we got home, he had also run a red light!

He experienced extreme vertigo imbalance and staggered into the living room that night. I got his cane, but he still had difficulty walking when he went to bed. The next morning, he was better and thought his pills had caused his dizziness. I didn't think so!

We tried another cooking lesson in the kitchen to get his mind on to a more positive subject, so we had a step-by-step run-down about planning tomorrow's menu. He set the crock pot out. I told him he would have to put the meatballs on to cook early so we could eat between one and two o'clock. He got a package of frozen spaghetti out of the freezer and put it in the refrigerator!

The next day we went over the lesson again to put the meatballs from Costco in the crockpot with a can of pasta sauce and a little water. I said, "Start it on high, then turn it to low. "After a while, he announced he was turning it down. When I checked the pot later, he had turned it clear off!

While the meatballs were back on cooking, Rick announced he was going down to pick a few things up and mail my letters that definitely needed to be at the mailbox before three o'clock. I had no idea what was so important that he had to leave before we ate, but he was gone for a long time, without his cell phone, and didn't get back until almost five o'clock. I was worried sick about him, had to deal with several phone calls, the dog barked when the doorbell rang, and my heart pounded after jumping off the couch to answer it. By the time Rick got home, I could hardly talk while trying to explain all that had transpired while he was gone. I hadn't eaten, and our lunch plans were long gone. He started telling me he'd gone here, gone there, and stopped to get the car washed, and of course, he didn't have a cell phone with him! Then I lost it, and the teardrops fell like rain!

The humidifier in my piano needed to be filled when the light was blinking. When it was installed, and we were shown how to fill the tank years before, Rick was on his hands and knees, seriously watching as though that was going to be his job in the future. However, that never happened until this particular day in March. I had the solution that goes into the water sitting on the dryer for two days and finally got around to starting the job. He offered to do it! I asked if he knew how to fill it, and he said he would figure it out. "Oh, no," I said while thinking at the same time, *"I'm not going to have that job botched up with water spilled all over the piano!"*

We had our taxes done, and, as usual, we both went for that appointment. Rick went for social reasons while I was trying to conduct business and get out of there. So, Rick proceeded to tell our tax man about the back surgery I had had where the orthopedic doctor chose to do a fusion so I wouldn't have to go back at any future date. But as the story was told, the doctor did fusions on all his patients. Far from accurate!

When Rick showed me how loose his wedding ring was, I put it away in a safe place. He didn't like me doing that and said he wouldn't lose it. Yea, right! He asked for it back and said he was going to get it resized, so I reminded him to get the gold they would take out. When he took it to the jewelry store, they told him they would incorporate the gold into the resizing cost! Sounded to me like they took advantage of him, but I wasn't there to witness their conversation.

We were leaving to go shopping, but he was in the kitchen getting a piece of candy before we left. When he heard me coming, he quickly swung around with the cane under his arm and shattered my apothecary glass that was on the counter. Glass flew from the counter to the floors in the kitchen and dining room, as well as the seats of the chairs. What a mess that was to clean up!

He drove through the ATM to get some cash, but he couldn't remember the PIN number again. I told him the steps on how to request the money, but somehow he failed to get a receipt. I think he inadvertently pressed "No!" On a previous occasion, when he got cash, the Visa statement came in showing he had gotten the money from that account instead of the checking account; that cost us a $12 fee!

One morning, he woke up with nausea and generally not feeling well after a bad night of jerking a lot. He ate a late breakfast, was dizzy before a late lunch, and was lying down most of the day.

There were more days like this as time ventured on.

We were out doing errands and came home to find the sliding glass door and screen wide open! As mentioned before, one of the last things on the agenda before we left was to take KQ out to potty, put him back in the kitchen, and close the gate. So far, that had been Rick's job.

A few days later, he started getting dizzy while bringing groceries into the house at about one o'clock. We ate lunch, and he was still dizzy. His cane was missing, and I went out to the car to see if it was there. In the meantime, I found him sitting at his desk on the phone, calling two places, asking if he had left his cane there. About three-twenty, I went back and found him still at his desk, sound asleep with the cell phone still in his hand. I checked his pulse, and he was breathing! About four forty-five, KQ woke him up, and he was still dizzy.

After that episode, I took him to the ER. They checked him out, ran a lot of tests that were normal, gave him a pill for vertigo that helped, and sent him home.

He felt better and went to the nursery several days later to pick up sprinkler supplies and some new Pyracantha bushes. I asked him how much the bill had come to so I could post it in the check register, but he didn't know. So, he tried to itemize everything in his head: two rolls of hose @ $3.69 each, etc. When I found the receipt inside the sack out in the garage, each roll of hose was $14.99! He managed to plant three of the four new bushes, but he was worn out before finishing the job, so I put a gallon of plant booster on each plant and cleaned the mess up for him.

We decided to take a little vacation down to Las Vegas for my birthday and stayed at one of the large, well-known resorts that host rodeos every year. At this point, I planned my own birthday celebrations! Rick decided he wanted valet and bell service this time, and I asked if he had money to give to the Bellboy. In a huff, he let me know he did! However, he never gave the "boy" anything when the luggage was delivered to our room.

We arrived on a weekday when it wasn't too crowded, and each of us found a slot machine in the same area but a short distance from one another. Eventually, I cashed out and found him sitting at a machine, sound asleep with his head hanging down. After I woke him up, he played it down like he really wasn't sleeping! Thankfully, he still had all his money!

He had just heard on the radio how dirty money is and asked, "Did you know that it carries all kinds of diseases, and it's recommended we wash our hands after handling it?" So, I asked him at least two times on this Vegas trip if he had washed his hands before eating. No, he hadn't!

Well, back home again with the usual routine of trying to cope with memory issues. He was advised by the neurologist to start using pain patches every day, so we bought a supply. I kept track of how many were used from a box and eventually discovered the same amount of patches still remained day after day. I asked if he was using the patches every day, and he replied, "Yes!" This was another example where I knew the answer before I asked the question, but it was my way of broaching the subject. I replied, "Every day?" He admitted, "Well, most days!" I responded saying, "I know you don't even use them most days!" He was sitting at his computer and just stared into space, not saying a word. And, at that point, I believe we were both steaming!

My blood was boiling because my plate was full trying to use every waking hour taking care of household chores, appointments, cooking, cleaning, and making sure his needs were met. Spending valuable time with an issue such as those patches and not being told the truth is something I had never tolerated too well. Telling the truth was ingrained in me at a very early age!

I believe his blood was also boiling because I was monitoring those patches, and he tried to cover up his failure to follow the instructions that he claimed he was capable of doing. It seemed he went into panic mode after the subject came up and tried to talk his way out of it. Caught once more!

Since he was still giving his own insulin shots, he asked one evening if I had any needles because he had run out.

I couldn't figure out how he didn't know when he took the last one out of his box, since all of his prescription meds and supplies were kept in his bathroom. Although I filled his weekly pill box, his insulin supplies were readily available and kept separately. My only request was for him to keep me advised when he was running low and needed refills, and this was a sure sign I needed to increase my "tracking" duties!

June rolled around and another fall happened out on the patio against a brick pillar. He didn't tell me until I noticed a bloody bandage on his elbow that night. The next day, I noticed a big knot with a dent resembling a hole in the middle of the area that had bled. It looked weird. This time, he said he was trying to drag the hose when it caught on something and then got uncaught, causing him to lose his balance.

Three days later, he made an unsuccessful attempt to walk on the decorative rock in the backyard again. His left knee and right shin were both skinned in addition to the already-injured elbow!

Ten days after that, he had been to the eye doctor and came home with both eyes dilated. He wasn't wearing any glasses and entered the RV for unknown reasons. Coming back out, he missed a step, toppled to the ground, and skinned his left knee again.

We made it to July that year, and I saw Rick on the ground after hearing a loud crash. He had been carrying a large plastic box into the house and must have missed a step, but when I asked what was going on, he said that he had just kicked the dog's water dish. I told him I'd seen him on the ground, but he wouldn't admit that he had fallen.

Shortly thereafter, he had an appointment with the cardiologist. Lab work looked good, and the doctor complimented Rick on having "good genes" but highly recommended he always use a cane because of Parkinson's. Rick beat around the bush about having Parkinson's and had no plans to depend on a cane!

After selling our truck and trailer a while back, we came across a small Class B Chinook motorhome that I was able to drive. Buying another RV was not in my plan, but it opened up an opportunity to make some short trips and break the monotonous routine we were stuck in. Rick spent a lot of time inside trying to figure out wiring configurations and tracing point A to point B of each wire.

Before I knew it, he informed me that none of the AC outlets in the RV worked after he drilled a hole for a cable and had accidentally cut a wire! So, we had to take it back to our RV repairman Jim to be repaired, and this was definitely not in the plan or the budget. WW III was about to begin!

Everything hit the fan about this time, with both of us vocally throwing darts at each other. He told me I hadn't had anything nice to say to him in the last year, that I never thanked him for doing anything around the house, that I called him all sorts of names, and that I looked at him like I hated him. Then I had my say-so, and I think we both felt better after unloading our frustrations. In my own defense, these accusations were as he perceived them that day and not how I felt I handled situations in the previous year. Calling him all sorts of names was absolutely untrue, and I definitely did not hate the man I had married. This disease was changing him into someone I didn't know anymore, and I was beginning to feel that I didn't know myself either. Sometimes, I would feel like I was being picked on, too, just as he said he was feeling. That's why we both needed to lean on Jesus more and more. Rick and I both believed that He was in charge of everything, and we trusted Him to get us through each day.

After things settled down, we took the RV in for evaluation and expected the worst when Jim called later with the shocking news that the only problem they discovered was that the GPS circuit breaker had tripped, and the wiring was just fine! That was worth a celebration, and happier days were upon us!

Rick wanted me to ask him nicely to do things, and he said he would be happy to do them! From then on, I tried to word my sentences very carefully so he would be able to "hear" me correctly.

This request actually put a smile on my face for him to come up with a simple solution that could improve our communication. I always thought I was asking him to do things nicely anyway, but I would try to do even better!

Since he had taken charge of the dog's evening feedings many years before, soaking his bowl afterwards was the last task to be done, so it would be clean the next morning. However, feeding the dog breakfast slowly became my job. More and more in the mornings, I found a dirty bowl with dried-up food. When I brought it to his attention again, his reply was that he remembered last night that he had forgotten to put water in the dish!

When he started carrying less money in his wallet, the credit cards should have been a consideration as well. We had two: one for internet and phone purchases and the other for local purchases that came straight from the checking account. He made two internet purchases and used the blue card that comes directly from the checking account. I didn't know that he no longer knew the difference between the two cards and refreshed his memory. He said, "OK," like he had never known!

The neurologist felt that his Parkinson's was getting worse at that point. She sent him to be tested for Lyme Disease because of all the complaints in one shin and the bottoms of both feet. That test came back negative.

She also referred him to an audiologist to have his hearing checked along with symptoms that may have been affecting his balance. The hearing test revealed his ears did not contribute to his balance problems, but he had high-pitch sound loss and was on the border of needing hearing aids. I knew at this stage that having the responsibility of hearing aids would be an impossible task for him to master, and I would run into opposition if I tried to assume the responsibility of helping. The audiologist performed a "DOT" test and concluded that Rick was only in the early stages of Parkinson's, if he even had the disease, because he passed! Physical therapy was recommended for his balance, so he started another round of that again.

As I kept my calendar updated with our busy schedule, I ran a copy for him to keep in his pocket so that he would not overbook appointments. I later wondered why I even bothered because it happened anyway!

In the meantime, his six-month appointment was due with the dermatologist. As usual, that doctor found places to be frozen by the little "gun" he always carried into the exam room! However, the doctor froze more on the face during this visit than he usually found, plus one place on an ear that would go in for a biopsy. Rick filled a prescription for a topical chemotherapy solution that would be applied to the scalp, ears, forehead, nose, and cheeks two times a day, and the face peel would last approximately three weeks. During this time, there were very few public outings since he felt miserable and looked like an alien from another planet! To add to his misery, the biopsy came back as a malignant basil cell that resulted in surgery on the top of his ear and took eleven stitches to close. The good news: He successfully recovered from both battles!

A week after the surgery, he got up from our rocker love seat and fell again. No injuries after this soft fall, but he said it was hard to get up after sitting so long.

Made a trip to InstaCare because he woke up with an earache. And since he had a problem with wax build-up in his ears, we both knew he probably needed to have it checked out. Sure enough, he felt lots better after we left!

An Ankle-Brachial Index Test (ABI) was done in a cardiologist's office to check for claudication arterial insufficiencies, and minimal was found. He followed up with a vascular doctor who confirmed there were minor insufficiencies, good pulse in the ankles, and no blockages from the heart to the ankles. The problem was neuropathy!

A podiatrist did an ultrasound on both feet where the left foot showed Plantar Fasciitis, a chunk of bone that was floating, and a groove that had filled in from a previous injury. A Cortisone shot in that foot gradually eased the pain enough for him to walk on it. The right foot was taped for two days to reduce inflammation, with heat applied every night. The sore tendons were possibly caused by ankle arthritis. The floating bone, in hindsight, may have been caused after he fell on New Year's Eve 1999 and suffered a badly-twisted ankle, or so we thought!

That particular New Year's Eve was widely publicized when the new year 2000, or Y2K, could possibly cause computer glitches with the turn of a new century. Everyone held their breath that there would be no major problems as the clocks struck midnight! With all the local celebrations happening to close out the twentieth century, another couple and we were in downtown St. George with hundreds of other people. As we walked through some grass, Rick's foot stepped in the wrong place at the wrong time!

We had reservations to camp at a Zion RV park, but Rick discovered a leak in one of the propane tanks the day before we were to leave, and we couldn't get it fixed in time to go. He told me to cancel the trip, so I did! He apologized for ruining our plans, but I didn't understand why he waited until the last day to check the tanks. Of course, he had an "essay" excuse to justify everything, and I chalked it up to bad judgement on his part. One conversation led to another, and he said to sell it.

My enthusiasm for travelling in that RV was gone because I had lost all confidence that something else might be overlooked before we travelled again.

When the RV was ready to sell, a couple came to see it. Rick had spent numerous hours making sure it was in tip-top condition for the viewing and went out before they arrived to double-check everything. When they arrived, the air conditioner wouldn't work! Rick admitted he didn't remember when he had last checked it but said he had checked everything before they arrived! We called Jim and took it in to be fixed. When they were troubleshooting the problem, they also found that the microwave wasn't working either! Jim also told Rick that too much force had been used to turn the propane valve "on" when it had been there for the leak prior to that. The couple was leaving town, so we lost that sale!

After those costly fixes, someone else came to see the RV, and that time, the generator wouldn't work! After that potential buyer left, the generator started right up. Good news: It finally did sell! Bad news: Rick started looking online for a small truck, which wasn't going to happen!

During a routine appointment with his primary doctor, it was recommended that Rick have a sleep study done since he seemed to be needing more pills to get a good night's sleep. During the study, he spent the night being monitored at their facility. The monitor left no questions unanswered, showing Rick had Sleep Apnea and stopped breathing twenty-seven times in sixty minutes for at least ten seconds each time. On the scale: 0-7 = normal, 6-14 = minimum, 15-30 = moderate, and over 30 = severe. A second study indicated that he had Central Sleep Apnea, where the brain didn't tell the body to breath. A third study was conducted using an ASV complex machine whereby it proved the first two studies were incomplete. The last study revealed that he had Moderate Obstructive Apnea but not Central Sleep Apnea, as the Titration Report performed during the second study indicated. The overall study concluded that A Fib may be causing oxygen deficiency in the brain, not Parkinson's. Further results showed his airway would collapse thirty-four events in a one-hour period.

After the second sleep study was completed, a CPAP machine was delivered and set up for Rick. He used this machine until it was decided after the third study he needed another machine with different air pressure. Rick used the new machine for a short period of time and decided the mask irritated his face; it was too noisy, and too much trouble to clean. So, this was the end of his CPAP experience.

Rick asked his neurologist for another memory test, which was completed. He received a score of thirty-one out of thirty-eight, down from thirty-five out of thirty-eight the year before.

Since it was the first of the month with checks written to pay bills, I had five envelopes on the counter ready to be taken to the post office. Rick was sitting at his desk and proceeded to tell me that so-and-so had sent us a check for a specific amount. I looked over to see what he was talking about, and in his hand was one of my outgoing checks, with the other hand holding the envelope he had ripped open! He usually was never interested in any mail and would toss it aside if I gave him something to open or read! So, why was he so interested in the mail that day?

One of the notes I wrote to myself after that episode read, *"Sometimes I wonder how close he is to Alzheimer's, when I know he's been in the Dementia stage for at least eight years. Today's incident with the mail was very unusual."*

We travelled to California in December to celebrate Christmas with family and watch one of our granddaughters perform in the Nutcracker. After leaving our favorite restaurant one evening, we were walking to the car in a semi-dark parking lot when Rick took a sudden dive and landed on his knees and right shoulder, sending his hat flying somewhere in the dark. I tried to quickly help him up, but he seemed quite disoriented and was dizzy when he stood up. He said he didn't hit his head, as he always tried to protect when he fell. I retrieved his hat, and he put it on but later said he didn't remember anything about the hat. Then, I noticed a "skid" mark on the hat that had to be scrubbed off after we returned home. So, I never really knew whether he hit his head or not.

Rick got sick Christmas morning, one week

after his fall, and said he hadn't felt right for the last three days! Two days later, I took him to InstaCare, where he received two prescriptions and was sent home to recover.

***

It was 2015, and I found myself filling Rick's weekly pill case, hoping he'd still manage to take his daily pills correctly. Time would tell! Just the next day, he forgot to take his nightly dose. Okay, maybe I'd need to start subtly looking over his shoulder—but if he thought I was spying, another fiasco might unfold!

I had to frequently update my Excel database of his medical conditions, prescriptions, supplements, allergies, medical history, and vaccines, as doctors were constantly tweaking his medications—either adding something new, discontinuing, or adjusting doses. I carried a copy with me to every doctor's appointment, so they could have the latest revision and see what the other doctors were prescribing. Rick kept a copy with his weekly pill case, and I had another stored in the "pill pantry." Rick often expressed his appreciation for my taking charge of this never-ending pill duty, and his thoughtful remarks were always well-received, just knowing he understood the effort involved.

We continued our appointments with the neurologist, but one particular visit earlier that year really caught me off guard. Rick seemed to come unglued, telling her that every time he wanted to go somewhere, I wanted to go too! When she suggested counseling, he claimed he had been wanting to go, but that I didn't want to see a counselor! This had never come up before—his answers seemed like they came from another planet! He even told her that when he got mad, he wouldn't talk to me. So, I came to the conclusion that he must be mad at me a lot, given how much time he spent alone in his room. I thought, *"I can't fix all his problems—I'm just his servant."* At that point, I didn't feel like talking to him either. After all, no conversation meant no arguments, right?

He even struggled to remember which of his eyes had macular degeneration, asking me for help recalling which one had been getting all the injections.

The movie "Still Alice" came out about a woman suffering from Alzheimer's. Rick insisted we go see it, and we could really relate to their Alzheimer's journey! I think it struck a deeper chord with him than he let on, knowing that he would probably be in that same condition someday.

In March 2015, Rick's neurologist referred him to a psychotherapist for counseling. Both of us attended sessions together and individually from May through September 2017. To start, Rick was evaluated by a neuropsychologist, undergoing a series of tests: Memory for Unrelated Sentences, the Wechsler Logical Memory Scale, the Hooper Visual Organization Test, Draw a Clock, the Boston Naming Test, Controlled Word Association Test, Peabody Picture Vocabulary Test, the Repeatable Battery for the Assessment of Neuropsychological Status, Wechsler Adult Intelligence Scale IV – Information and Similarties, Raven Standard Matrices Test, Wisconsin Card Sorting Test, Zung Depression Scale, and Patient Rated Anxiety Scale.

At the conclusion of Rick's testing, counselling was recommended because of the high probability of interpersonal misperception due to the discrepancy between his reasoning ability and his memory impairment. For example, he scored well in some areas, like drawing a clock. He functioned in the bright, normal range for verbal fluency, but his conversations were inaccurate when he confused events in time. This created a problematic picture in that people would overestimate his ability and become surprised by his difficulty with memory and executive functioning, which was apt to cause resentment on his part and confusion on the part of those he was closest to. After the tests were completed, the results confirmed Frontal Lobe Dementia with Parkinson's and depression.

At last, we had confirmation of what we had been dealing with. It was a bittersweet revelation—while it was a relief to know I wasn't imagining things, the reality that things weren't going to improve hit hard.

We both attended the first counseling appointment, where she recommended Rick get an EEG. She also suspected he might have hit his head when he fell off the RV ladder, possibly losing consciousness briefly. He admitted it was possible. Then, there was the incident where he tripped over a curb at Michael's, hitting his forehead on the concrete, which could have caused further damage. She explained that even a jolt to the brain with an "energy" force could do some damage.

Counseling gave both of us a chance to vent and unload years of built-up frustration. This referral turned out to be one of the best decisions, offering help we desperately needed—and should have sought long before communication became so difficult.

Still, there were no overnight improvements. When my birthday approached, I didn't ask questions when Rick said he was going shopping. Three hours later, he came home, carrying a small, card-sized sack down the hall. A card is exactly what I got for my birthday—along with the "promise" of a concert the following month. After several attempts for us to find the box office open to buy tickets, we finally enjoyed a lovely evening with the Southwest Symphony Orchestra about two weeks later.

Just before payday, Rick informed me he was out of cash and needed to withdraw some. When I reminded him payday was on Friday and asked if he could wait, he snapped at me, saying he shouldn't have to wait until after Friday to get money! Then, on the first of the month, while balancing the bank statement, I noticed he had withdrawn $100 from the

ATM before my birthday. I had no idea what he did with that money, especially since he claimed to be broke by the end of the month. He certainly didn't spend it on concert tickets because when we went to the box office, I used my credit card!

Our church was gearing up for its annual rummage sale, and donations were due the following week. Rick started pulling items from drawers, searching his closet, taking things off shelves, and making a fairly large pile on the floor. But that's as far as he got. When the day arrived to load the car, his pile was still sitting there untouched. It frustrated me that he had days to prepare but never finished the project. Since he wasn't ready to donate his things, he informed me that he'd just put them in a box and donate them somewhere else.

I also started noticing how much Rick was mimicking what others were doing. For instance, if he saw me snacking while I worked at the desk, he'd immediately go to the kitchen and grab the same snack—even though he had already made several trips to the kitchen for other snacks. There was a friendly member at our church who greeted people each Sunday, and Rick once commented on how good a public relations (PR) man he was for the church. The very next Sunday, Rick took it upon himself to get up, shake hands, and flash his best smile at everyone, pouring on the charm. But by the following week, he didn't even attempt to greet anyone. When he noticed this same PR guy had grown a goatee, Rick decided to grow one too—but thankfully, he eventually shaved it off!

One day, we decided to take a short drive to Zion for lunch, which was less than an hour away. Before leaving town, we stopped to fill the gas tank. Then, Rick suggested stopping at our favorite drive-thru for a burger "to tide us over." I looked at him and said, "Seriously?" and he responded with a firm "Yes." Honestly, food was always his number-one priority!

Speaking of priorities, I came home one day after getting a cortisone shot in a painful hip. Expecting a bit of sympathy, I greeted him with "Hi" as I walked through the door. But instead of asking how my appointment went, he immediately launched into a rundown of the news he was watching on TV!

We shopped for some friends each week who lived in different assisted-living facilities. We'd keep their separate shopping lists organized in the cart and on the conveyor belt, and I made sure the bags stayed separated in the car. It all went smoothly until one day when Rick wanted to place the groceries on the conveyor belt himself. Assuming he knew the routine we always followed, I trusted him to handle it while I headed to the register to pay for each order. Unfortunately, I wasn't paying close enough attention and discovered too late that all the groceries had been mixed together. The checker had no idea we had two separate orders. Fortunately, there weren't too many items, and I was able to sort things out and straighten up the payment, but it certainly taught me a lesson!

One day, we left the house for a doctor's appointment, and Rick forgot his wallet. Then, he left his glasses behind at the doctor's office. Later, he fell in the pharmacy parking lot, scraping his elbow and knee, and ended up with a sore ankle. By far, it wasn't his best day!

Meanwhile, Rick's ophthalmologist performed another routine exam after his eyes were dilated from his recent visit to the retinal specialist. The doctor scanned his eyes for glaucoma, a concern due to the injections Rick had been receiving for his macular degeneration. Thankfully, it only showed very early stages.

Rick expressed concern to his retinal specialist in August that he thought he had been seeing more wavy lines in his right eye—the "good" eye, not the one receiving the injections. Six weeks later, during the next exam, dry macular degeneration (MD) was detected in his right eye, though fortunately, no injections were needed at that time for the dry MD.

But then, in October, Rick woke up to find he had completely lost vision in his right eye. His retina doctor saw him immediately and discovered that Rick had suffered a massive sub-retinal hemorrhage, which had completely destroyed the retina. Vitrectomy surgery followed without success, and he was declared legally blind two months later. The doctor said it was the worst case he had ever encountered in his career and suspected that the blood thinners Rick had been taking were a contributing factor, although it was hard to prove. His driving days were officially over.

With Rick no longer able to drive, the complaints about my driving gradually disappeared. He actually became a more pleasant passenger, enjoying the scenery with what little vision he still had in his left eye. I couldn't help but feel this was an example of how the Lord resolved the driving issues between us.

As 2015 drew to a close after countless medical appointments, we still weren't done. Rick had to visit the dermatologist again. During a routine semi-annual checkup, several areas were treated with that infamous freezing gun the doctor always carried. Then, just before Christmas, Rick had surgery to remove a basal cell carcinoma, known to grow under the surface 90% of the time. It took fifteen stitches to close the wound near his eyebrow, but he recovered well from that experience, too. Every time he went through one of those procedures, he was such a trooper—so brave!

Rick's Atrial Fibrillation (A Fib) was described by his primary doctor as sounding like popcorn. Over the years, the various blood thinners he had taken caused different reactions. So, what now?

The cardiologist informed us about a device called the Watchman. While not as effective as blood thinners, it was proving to be a good alternative. Rick was encouraged that this might be the solution to prevent future blood clots and strokes caused by A Fib. However, he needed approval from his retinal doctor before moving forward with the procedure.

***

The new year, 2016, began with Rick getting his stitches out from the cancer surgery, and thankfully, the incision looked good! But before January ended, he tripped over one of the desk legs in the office and fell. A couple of days later, while using a screwdriver, he cut the palm of his hand. Adjusting to his new vision loss was not going well. He kept trying to do the things he had always done, either refusing to acknowledge his new limitations or simply forgetting he needed to be more careful. I couldn't always tell what was going through his mind or what he was thinking.

Rick was often bored and wanted to find more fun things to do. Though he wasn't much of a social planner, he was always happy to join in once someone else made the plans. However, during the many idle hours when he seemed to be doing nothing, his mind was still thinking of something.

He shocked me one day with a bright idea and all the reasons why we should do it. He said, "Let's move someplace else!"

I listened, processed what he said, slept on it, prayed about it, and couldn't find a good reason to say no. There were things about our house that I didn't particularly like, and it seemed like maybe this was the right time to make a move while Rick could somewhat still help. One big factor was the scorpions we kept finding in the house, even with regular pest control visits. Plus, the floor plan wasn't ideal—getting from the garage to the kitchen was inconvenient, and all the bedrooms were on one side of the house. After much thought, I agreed that it was a good time for a change.

We soon began making plans to downsize and sort through things we no longer needed. While I couldn't expect a lot of help from Rick due to his physical condition, he still had strong arms, and I was grateful for the strength he could offer.

As we searched from St. George to Las Vegas for a home that met our needs, we also prepared our house to go on the market. We held another successful garage sale, packed up household goods, and even rented a storage unit to temporarily hold some of our belongings.

We searched online, found a realtor locally and in Las Vegas, eliminated many houses, and toured quite a few. Once our house went on the market, it sold quickly, and the clock started ticking. Soon enough, we bought our current home in a city near St. George. Move day was set for Friday the 13th!

Since Rick was born on Friday the 13th, he always considered it his lucky day. As for me, I wasn't so sure, but I hoped it would bring us good luck for the move. The first red flag came when the moving van arrived—and was obviously too small to fit all our furniture in one trip. They assured us, "No problem. We'll just make two trips!" By the end of those trips, they had nicked some furniture, door frames, and walls—nothing a little Old English and paint couldn't fix, but still, it wasn't the luckiest Friday the 13th I'd ever had!

We made many changes to our new home both before and after the move. Contractors were constantly coming in and out, sometimes bumping into each other, while Rick was always there to supervise and offer advice. What had once been a rental soon became a home. We felt our prayers had been answered in finding this house—it was the perfect choice for us and a refreshing change. It felt like a new beginning, giving us something to focus on besides ourselves.

One landscaper, while discussing the backyard he was about to transform, commented to me that Rick's dementia was quite noticeable. Rick had been talking to him about the yard, repeating himself while trying to explain something the landscaper had just explained to him. After that, the landscaper mentioned he would listen to me in the future.

Before the move, however, a dental appointment in February brought dreaded news. Rick still had his wisdom teeth, but two of them had cavities. Two of his molars, which had partial root canals, were affecting the wisdom teeth. There were three options: pull the molars, get a bridge, or opt for implants. To add to that, he had an infection that would need to be treated with antibiotics. Rick decided to have the two molars pulled.

With no dental insurance, this was another shock to our finances.

Rick relinquished his driver's license and received an identification card in April. Giving up that license and replacing it with an ID card was one of his most depressing days. Once he tucked the new card into his wallet, it felt final, but that didn't stop him from sitting behind the wheel again later, which I only heard about after the fact!

About two weeks later, he had a fall on the patio and bent his glasses. The frames dug into the area near his eyebrow where stitches had recently been removed, so butterfly bandages were applied to stop the bleeding. He also scratched his knee, and one hand was very unhappy.

I took Rick to the ER in mid-May after his hip became quite painful. After undergoing an exam and filling enough test tubes to satisfy the lab, no specific diagnosis was given. A few days later, he received a cortisone shot from his primary care physician. And in case you're wondering—yes, he had my deepest sympathy for that painful hip, which was more than he gave me for mine!

Retinal appointments continued regularly, and a yearly ophthalmology checkup confirmed he still had mild glaucoma. Rick still held out hope that his right eye's vision would improve, despite occasional bleeding. Laser treatments were discussed, but with no guarantees, he decided against that option.

Arrangements were made through the local Red Rock Center for Independence to purchase items specifically designed for the visually impaired. Rick was very encouraged by the selection and immediately chose a talking watch, a special pair of glasses for watching TV, and a powerful magnifying glass.

They also contacted the Veteran's Administration (VA) office in Salt Lake City to get Rick registered for benefits. As promised, we received a call from Ms. Brown, who became our VA contact. She sent us an application through the mail, which I filled out and returned for final approval. After the lengthy application process, Rick's approval came through, and he proudly received his official Veteran's ID card. Carrying that card in his wallet helped soften the blow of losing his driver's license.

The VA Library for the Visually Impaired in Salt Lake City provided Rick with a recorder and sent audiobooks regularly. He could choose a few books at a time from a catalog that arrived several times a year. The books brought him a lot of joy, though there was one recurring problem—not the books' fault, but he often fell asleep in the middle of many stories!

In August, we traveled to Midvale, Utah, for Rick to receive the Watchman device, which was a Left Atrial Appendage Closure, performed by the only doctor in Utah offering the procedure at the time. Since it was a five-to-six-hour trip, we booked a hotel as close to the hospital as we could get and had no idea why it was so difficult to find one with vacancies when I made the reservation.

The hotel had recently been renovated and just reopened. Our room was at the end of a long hallway, then down another long hallway, and the very last one on the left. The window was so close to the sidewalk and a busy street that it felt like you could almost reach out and touch it. We managed to get through the first night despite the noise and my growing sense of insecurity, but there was no way I was going to spend another night in that room, especially knowing I'd be alone for part of our stay!

The following morning, I went to the front desk and politely explained our situation, including the noisy and isolated room we had been given. The desk clerk must have had a soft spot hearing my plea for help, because she upgraded us to a large, safe suite at no extra charge for the rest of our stay. She earned a well-deserved tip for that!

Rick arrived at the hospital for his pre-op visit after lunch. When I mentioned to the doctor what an adventure it had been finding a hotel that week, he apologized and confessed that he hadn't realized a big convention was in town when he scheduled Rick's surgery. The pre-op went smoothly, and they confirmed they'd be ready for him early the next morning. After the appointment, we drove to Gardner Village in West Jordan to explore the shops and enjoy an early dinner before heading back to the hotel.

The big day finally arrived! It had been over a year since Rick's cardiologist first mentioned the Watchman device, so he had given it a lot of thought. He was excited that this would be the safest option for him. After the procedure, Rick was kept overnight and discharged the following afternoon. We spent one more night in our deluxe suite before heading home the next day.

Back home, our usual routine resumed, though "normal" rarely meant what I expected! Rick had a knack for keeping things exciting, not with flowers or love notes, but with other surprises. Believe me, it wasn't unusual to find frozen waffles in the refrigerator or to learn he'd had a peanut butter sandwich before breakfast! He also struggled with remembering the steps for leaving the dog inside when we went out. For the third and final time, we came home to find the dog outside and the sliding glass door wide open!

Rick's neurologist adjusted his medications, discontinuing one to see if his Parkinson's symptoms worsened. It became very clear that without Carbidopa, his symptoms did increase—he moved more slowly, stumbled while walking, and shuffled his feet more. With this noticeable change, Parkinson's was definitely confirmed, and Rick resumed taking Carbidopa.

After months of delay, partly due to insurance only covering one PET scan of the brain in a lifetime unless cancer was involved, Rick decided to have the scan. He felt it was important to know what was going on in his brain, even if it meant using his one-time insurance benefit. The results confirmed early-stage Alzheimer's, which, although not surprising, was still disappointing. It was a bit shocking to hear it was "early-stage," as it felt like we had been living with these challenges for a very long time.

Once the results were in, Rick and I discussed the next steps with his Primary Physician. Rick chose to stop seeing the neurologist and asked this doctor to manage his care for diabetes, Parkinson's, and Alzheimer's. The doctor suspected Rick might have Parkinson's Plus and agreed to take over all his care, which would help prevent prescriptions from overlapping between different specialists.

Rick had follow-up visits with his cardiologist after receiving the Watchman device. He was monitored closely as he was weaned off his blood thinner and started on a new medication called Plavix. Protime tests were discontinued, and a Trans-esophageal

Echocardiogram (TEE) was performed a month later to confirm that the device was in place and his heart was functioning well.

Rick's appetite, however, remained very good—perhaps too good! By September, the shirts I had bought for him in June were already too tight. It was time for a pep talk, but these conversations usually went in one ear and out the other, as he didn't want to hear it. Since one of my many duties was to keep his wardrobe clean, organized, and mended, I felt entitled to defend those clothes!

After we returned from lunch one day, I fixed us some carb-smart ice cream, but Rick immediately headed to the pantry for some nuts. I told him that if he wanted to lose weight, some snacks had to go. He agreed, saying, "OK, but nuts are good." But that wasn't the end of it—after the nuts, he went for popcorn! So, I didn't fix dinner that night. Of course, he made himself his favorite: a peanut butter and jelly sandwich.

Later, I had a conversation with him about how I had a problem with people who didn't care about their appearance and that something needed to change. It didn't seem to make much of a difference, but at least I got it off my chest.

We had a cement patio poured, and a small corner was left smooth for our initials and KQ's paw print. Rick had our four-legged Yorkie on a leash to keep him away from the wet concrete, but suddenly, KQ broke free and ran all over the fresh cement. Oh my, oh my gosh! Panic set in. I quickly called the contractor after rescuing our naughty dog. One of the crew members returned and smoothed out all the paw prints. I was so grateful that he came so quickly that I gave him a generous tip for cutting into his off-duty time. However, when the invoice arrived, there was an extra charge for the service, making it another costly mishap!

***

A couple of weeks later, another area of concrete was ready to be poured, and the gates to the backyard had temporarily been removed. With no gates, we had to take KQ outside and make sure he didn't wander over to that side of the house. One particular night, however, Rick took him out and realized he had to go to the bathroom too. So, he went back inside, leaving KQ outside in the dark.

When I asked Rick where the dog was, he casually said, "He's out back, and he's fine."

But when I went outside to check on KQ, I didn't see him right away. Then, I noticed something moving near the back fence. I called for him but got no response, so I grabbed a flashlight and walked towards that moving object. There he was—completely spooked, frozen in place, and refusing to move or come to me. He kept looking back at the porch as if waiting for Rick, who had clearly abandoned him! The only way I could coax him back inside was by bribing him with ice cream, and once he heard those two little words, he came a runnin!

After the new landscaping was completed, we discovered a drainage issue in the backyard. Rick thought he could fix it like he did at our previous house, but I wasn't so sure that would work here. I shared my thoughts and left him to mull it over. Later, I asked if he was actively coming up with a plan, and what I got was an "essay" answer. In reality, there was no plan, and it was clear the conversation needed to end right there.

Eventually, Rick wanted me to go outside so we could discuss it further. He asked for my thoughts again, and I showed him my ideas. Of course, he had his rebuttals, and we still weren't making any progress. Frustrated, I told him I'd call a gutter professional for advice. Much later, Rick—acting as if it were his idea—suggested I contact the gutter experts. In the end, we hired someone to dig three trenches and install drains to direct rainwater to the back of our property.

One morning, I went outside to sit on the patio and drink my coffee. Rick came out with KQ, and I mentioned that KQ didn't need to be on a leash as long as we were both there to keep an eye on him. I went inside to grab my garden tools and do some trimming on our new fruitless plum tree. Afterward, I put the tools and trimmings away in the garage. When I came back, Rick was standing in the yard, looking around. I asked where KQ was, and Rick said he was looking for him. I immediately checked the side yard, where the gates were still down, and sure enough, KQ was out in the front yard! I brought him back to the patio, but it was clear—Rick wasn't able to "see" where the dog was, and I needed to stop relying on him to keep an eye on things. Rick also needed to start admitting when he couldn't "see" something instead of pretending he could.

Rick asked me if I had a radio on somewhere. I told him I didn't but suggested maybe he had left his on. He said he hadn't because the batteries were dead, despite the fact that I had just replaced them two weeks prior! I went into his room and found his audiobook recorder still playing. I turned his radio on, raised the volume, and, lo and behold, it worked just fine!

This year was filled with more misunderstandings, miscommunications, and misinterpretations than all the previous years combined. We both had our bad moments, but it was especially tough when they happened at the same time. It was Fall 2016, and we had settled into the new house, with most of the remodeling complete. Of course, not every moment was chaotic—there were times when things were calm and peaceful, too. But all it took was one question or comment to turn everything upside down in a split second!

One day, I was chatting with a friend on the phone in the office, and it was just some light-hearted chit-chat I planned to tell Rick about later. We were talking about an over-the-counter item from the health store, so I got up to grab mine from the medicine cabinet. As I turned around to leave the office and enter the kitchen, I caught Rick eavesdropping! He took off as quickly as his feet could move, heading straight for his bedroom. I followed him and asked, "Is there something I can help you with?" With guilt written all over his face, he simply said, "No." When I got off the phone, I let him know exactly what I thought about his eavesdropping. He started to deny it, but I told him not to even go there—I had caught him red-handed. Later that night, before bed, he apologized and promised he'd never do that again.

Rick was also having increasing trouble with his cell phone. He started punching the wrong buttons or calling the wrong person who was on his contact list. Sometimes, he'd miss calls because the phone was in his pocket, and he wouldn't hear it ring. Other times, he fumbled with the phone, trying to answer it. The caller was usually me! When I was out running errands, I often called to check in on him, but he struggled with even the simplest functions, like retrieving voicemails or turning the phone on and off. Eventually, anyone who tried to call him would just call me instead.

Whenever I received a call meant for Rick, I'd hand him the phone instead of putting it on speaker since most of those calls were from his Lodge friends. But even then, he'd hold the phone too far away, talking "to" the phone instead of "into" the mouthpiece. His confusion with the phone grew worse, yet he insisted on having his own with a separate number. At one point, I was tempted to buy him a toy phone to play with!

***

CHAPTER 04 | Making Choices

By the end of 2016, Rick seemed to get everything mixed up. We made a trip to the nursery to get a bag of Pay Dirt for the new oak tree in the backyard and bags of topsoil for the flower beds. I was inside paying while he stepped outside to show the employee what we were buying so he could load the trunk. He had already seen which bags we were buying before I went inside, so he pointed out the ones to load. One problem: the six bags of topsoil were the wrong ones! That mistake was corrected, and he apologized to the man.

When we got home, he unloaded the trunk and put the heavy bags from the nursery on the side of the house, planning to fill the hole with Pay Dirt before the oak tree arrived. But after lunch, he sat in his favorite chair watching TV and completely forgot about finishing the work outside until I had to remind him. It wasn't fun that I often had to give him a firm boost to get things done, and it felt like he was acting more like an obstinate teenager. That isn't the kind of person I wanted to be, and I didn't like feeling forced to take any kind of action to get things done.

At this time, the first one in the kitchen took on the chore of feeding KQ. Rick opened a new container of Cesar's dog food to feed KQ breakfast. I had fed the dog the night before and had already opened a new one; the other half was in the refrigerator. He said he had used the last of the food the previous day, but that was in the morning. He claimed he didn't see any other food in the refrigerator, but he had put the other half of his container right next to it! I asked him how he could not have seen it when he had just put the other half in the refrigerator, but he didn't want to talk about it.

He attended a Lodge meeting around Thanksgiving after I drove him to the Lodge, and another member promised to bring him home. However, the driver had never been to our house. On their way back, Rick couldn't remember the street we lived on or how to get home. He did, however, remember the house number. The driver's GPS guided them in the right direction, and Rick made it home! This incident alarmed him enough to realize how much his memory had declined, and he later discussed his concern with the doctor. That was when he received the results of his PET scan, showing early Alzheimer's.

He had been having difficulty taking his blood sugar in the mornings and said he had to take it twice to get a reading. When I offered to help, I discovered he only had one strip left in a bottle of fifty that was new just a month earlier. He was going to run out before a new prescription was due to be filled! I noticed that only two of his fingers had numerous pricks on them, and he told me he only used those two to check his sugar. I explained that he needed to use both hands and alternate fingers!

We also had a discussion about his pain pills. I asked if he was taking them to sleep or because he was in pain. He said he would usually take one around three in the morning because he was awake at that time. I disagreed, telling him that taking one that late at night—or, more accurately, that early in the morning when he'd be waking up soon, didn't make sense.

Later, he told me he was going to try to stop taking the pain pills altogether because he thought maybe he shouldn't mix them with the other medications he was on. A good point, but the doctor was aware of all his medications and had said the dosage wasn't high enough to cause concern. The pain pills were for his neuropathy, not for sleep!

A few days later, he took his blood sugar, and it was one-ninety-two. I took it again, and it was one-fifty-six. He insisted the damn machine was the problem, not him! So, I used the control solution to double-check the machine and found it was working just fine. When I asked if he had taken a pain pill, he admitted he had taken one around three-thirty that morning. After breakfast, I caught him getting a muffin out of the freezer just as I walked back into the kitchen. I asked him why he was eating a muffin when his sugar was already too high, and his excuse was, "It's only one-fourth of a muffin!" It didn't matter how big it was, so I told him he had to take some responsibility for his health. All he did was eat whatever he wanted whenever he wanted. If he had been my kid, I would have said, "No muffin," but he still insisted on being in control. He resented my interference, and it could easily start an argument.

If he was thirsty, do you think he would get a glass of water? No. He would head straight to the fridge in the garage and grab a can of soda. He was addicted to Cactus Coolers—loved those the most—and would throw them in the grocery cart whenever he shopped with me. It became such a habit, and I would sometimes count him drinking up to three a day!

Finally, I asked him what he wanted me to do about these out-of-control habits, and he said he didn't know. I asked, "Do you want me to nag and bitch at you?" and he just said, "I don't know!" I came back with, "One of these days, I'm going to say, 'Enough is enough'." Then he told me he would eat only what I told him to eat. I quickly replied, "Oh no. You're not going to put that burden back on me. I've heard that before, and I've heard that line too many times." And once again, nothing was accomplished!

There was a special on TV about Glen Campbell's Alzheimer's journey that Rick watched with full attention. He knew Glen's condition could be a preview of what his own future might look like, but he never wanted to bring up the subject or talk about it. That was just Rick—he wouldn't dive into difficult subjects and, most of the time, tried to avoid discussing anything painful or unpleasant.

As another year came to an end, we had our annual California trip planned to visit relatives and see our granddaughter in another performance of *The Nutcracker*. The trip went well, but just before Christmas, I came down with Type A Flu and ended up in the ER on Christmas Eve!

Rick had a dream one night after we'd had an especially difficult day that left both of us in tears. He tried to explain it in vivid detail and said he wanted us to move—specifically, into an Assisted Living Facility. He described one facility, but I was pretty sure he actually meant another one closer to the mall, and that was the one he meant. Since that wasn't the one he was describing, I began to picture the one he described in my mind. Somewhere along the way, I realized we weren't even on the same page.

Then he admitted that he thought we would enjoy one other's company more if we saw less of each other! He went on to say he'd been listening to one of his audiobooks that explained both his condition and mine as a caregiver. Finally, he brought one of his inner thoughts out in the open and was ready to talk about it. It was good to hear him share and consider possible options for what had felt like an impossible situation. Still, moving again wasn't in my plans! But just having an open conversation about something new was refreshing, and he even seemed in a cheerful mood at the thought of going someplace else to live!

As the year came to a close, I was exhausted—my energy level had hit rock bottom with all the holiday preparations, traveling, and recovering from the flu. We found ourselves butting heads in so many conversations that it became almost unbearable for both of us. It felt like I was expected to carry on with everything as usual, but I couldn't rely on much help from Rick. And with no fault of his own, any time he tried to help, it ended up with me having to assist him! There had to be a better way, and we needed help to get through this!

***

In 2017, a call to the St. George Memory Matters office was truly life-saving and was a positive turning point. Rick was enrolled in a class one day a week for four hours, which included lunch and activities designed for people living with dementia. He made new friends quickly and became a favorite among the staff, thanks to his jovial personality. One activity he especially enjoyed and excelled in was their painting class, led by a professional local artist who volunteered his time and talents to these enthusiastic students! Even with Rick's low vision, he managed to create two beautiful paintings that were exhibited at a local art gallery. His first masterpiece was of the Zion mountains, and his second was an Aspen forest.

There were other activities aimed at stimulating the brain, like word games on the blackboard, but Rick didn't enjoy those as much—he couldn't get close enough to clearly see the blackboard. However, he loved the balloon toss and still managed to slam a powerful punch! Those four hours always seemed to go by quickly, and they were a refreshing break for both of us. This became our routine for two years, until another life-changing event occurred.

I was also introduced to the Five Counties Area Agency on Aging in St. George through the Memory Matters office. A representative interviewed me over the phone and later visited our home to interview both of us to see if we qualified for a grant to help with some of our expenses. Fortunately, we were approved for some financial assistance towards Rick's Memory Matters classes for a limited time, which was a great relief.

In addition, I pursued another option to see if something could help with Rick's neuropathy and possibly even his brain issues. He started a series of treatments, three times a week for a total of twenty-three visits, at the Pain, Injury, and Brain Center in St. George. Their micro-current therapy aimed to detoxify the cells and allow nutrients to enter while also focusing on diet and water intake. While there wasn't an overnight improvement that we could see, we remained hopeful that it would improve his quality of life—and maybe it did! Rick was never much of a water drinker and still didn't drink enough, even when he tried. As for diet, what diet?!

Our calendar became so packed over the next few months, and sometimes, we had two or three appointments in a single day. One dental visit required a deep cleaning and filling of a cavity next to a tooth he had pulled last year. At the audiologist, we learned there was some hearing loss in his right ear, but more significant loss in the left ear since his last test. The retina doctor said the right eye looked worse this time, though surprisingly, the left eye had actually improved! Rick couldn't see out of his right eye anyway, but the doctor could tell from the behind-the-eye photos taken that day. He was also hopeful that the micro-current therapy might improve the little eyesight Rick had left.

This busy schedule was both exhilarating and exhausting, but keeping our minds active and moving forward felt like a healthy change. Keeping Rick engaged in activities that might help him improve was definitely a step in the right direction.

If we left for an appointment before lunch, he knew that meant we got to go out to eat afterwards! If we went to a restaurant, the menu was like a blank check for him to eat anything his heart desired. A buffet was even better—until the time came when I had to start carrying his tray and could serve him smaller portions. That gave me a little control over portion size and keeping his meals somewhat balanced, but he wasn't too happy about losing that bit of freedom. If we left home after lunch, he would often say, "I'm hungry!" Hint, hint: "I want to stop and get some ice cream, etc.!"

Although he was still getting around without using the cane like his doctor had recommended, his walking became slower, and his feet shuffled more with every step.

A Lodge brother brought him home after a meeting one night. Rick walked up the walkway and knocked for me to let him in. I went to the door and asked, "Is that you?" No answer. I asked again, and still no answer. I looked through the peephole and could see his silhouette near the front of the garage. He turned around and walked back up the walkway toward the front door again. I thought, *"Wait a minute, didn't I just hear him knock?"* I opened the door, and there he was! He explained that after knocking, he wasn't sure if it was our house, so he went back out front to double-check!

The next morning, I was eating breakfast when he got up, and I had already cooked bacon for both of us. He started fixing an English muffin to pop into the toaster, so I finished up and left the kitchen to get ready for the day. Less than five minutes later, he came in and asked if I could help with his egg. He walked over to the stove and was staring at the microwave, as if trying to figure out how to use it. I noticed the skillet on a burner with an egg already cracked into it, but the burner wasn't on. I asked if he was trying to cook the egg in the microwave, and he looked confused, like he suddenly realized the microwave wasn't what he needed. When I asked why he had broken the egg into a cold skillet, he said, "I thought it was hot!" So, I cooked the egg for him.

As I started cleaning up, I noticed how dirty the cube of butter was and asked if he had used the whole cube to grease the skillet. He said, "Well, yes!" That's when I gave him a quick lesson on using butter, telling him to cut off what he needed next time and put that in the skillet. Just another normal day for us!

He tried to help by unloading the clean dishes from the dishwasher, but he wasn't putting them where they belonged. He kept opening cupboard doors, but he couldn't seem to remember where anything went. Finally, I asked him not to unload the clean dishes anymore. I told him that just loading the dirty ones would be more helpful!

There are a lot of boulders behind our fenced yard in a common area. One day, he pointed them out and said they were new. I told him they had been there for a long time, but he insisted they were new! To settle his confusion, I found a picture on my phone of him sitting on the patio with the boulders in the background. That seemed to satisfy his confusion.

He woke up with the idea to rearrange his bedroom again, so that became our project for the day! He knew exactly how he wanted everything to be moved, whether it fit or not. With my help and approval, we managed to move the heavy furniture around. Then, I took pictures off one wall and hung them on another. The biggest task for him was unplugging all the computer wires from the armoire and trying to remember how to plug them back in correctly. Sometimes, he couldn't quite figure it out, and we had to call for outside help to get everything hooked up again. Less than three months later, we ended up doing it all over again!

He also became the proud owner of a Jitterbug cell phone, hoping it would solve the problems he was having with his old, more "sophisticated" phone—which was actually one of the most simplified models available. I thought he'd be able to master the easy instructions once I had entered all his contacts, but months went by, and it proved otherwise. Half the time, he would leave it in his room, and I'd find it later with no charge. He would tell me the charger wasn't working, and I discovered more than once that he hadn't placed it in the charger correctly. Other times, I'd turn his phone on and see missed calls or messages that he never noticed. This phone was turning out to be more work than it was worth, and I had a feeling it would eventually end up turned off for good.

Trying to keep up with all his needs and wants started to overwhelm me again. The psychotherapist we were still seeing suggested I write him a letter and tell him everything that was on my mind:

"Dear Rick, *March 2017*

This letter is being written to you in order for me to get some things off my chest. It is not meant for you to read nor hear because I realize the issues bothering me about you are not deliberate on your part. I DO know that your brain is not at one-hundred percent anymore, and I know there's not much you can do about it. The man I married has long gone, the man I could depend on to understand my conversations isn't here anymore, the man who could understand my moods has disappeared, and the man who knew when to step up to the plate is lost.

I am trying to be patient, understanding, and thoughtful in your declining years. I don't mean to be short with you when you don't get it, and I don't want to become the kind of person I can't stand myself. I am struggling with my own age-related problems while still trying to be the same young, energetic person I used to be.

I miss the man I married, but I know he will never be there for me again. I know you'd like him to be there, but I don't think you realize he's really passed on. You only know the person who is here today, and you want him to be happy doing all the fun things he likes to do. Just like a little kid, he will get outside and work if I nag and keep reminding him that there are jobs to be done, but "work" is only a four-letter word to you now. You'd rather do something fun, or put something together that takes you forever nowadays, or eat another meal. With your low vision problems, it's really hard for you to see things that I still take for granted that you can still see. Sometimes, I need to repeat myself over and over again to remind you that I want you to do something. It has gotten to the point that I have to go behind you to see if it's done right. I can't even rely on you anymore, so I am learning to do things myself while trying really hard to keep quiet.

I am so very sorry all these medical problems have

taken a hold on you in the years when we had planned to enjoy retirement. I know it wasn't your plan to become disabled and have to depend on me for so many things. Who would have thought? This is the Lord's plan and we know this. We don't always understand the whys and what-fors, but we have to take one day at a time and follow His plan. I pray that the Lord will keep me strong and healthy so I can always be here for you."

Rick had some routine blood work done, and his hemoglobin (HGB) and hematocrit (HCT) counts came back too high. He was diagnosed with a condition called Polycythemia, which occurs when the body produces too many red blood cells. As a result, he needed monthly visits to the Phlebotomy Department at the hospital, where they would withdraw 500 ml (or 0.5 liters) of blood if his HGB was over fifteen and/or his HCT was over forty-five. These visits had to be scheduled within seventy-two hours of his lab test. So, our routine became: go to the lab on Wednesday, pick up a hard copy of his report on Thursday, and, if the numbers were too high, head to the hospital for phlebotomy on Friday. If the numbers were normal, I'd cancel the appointment and reschedule for the next month.

Due to HIPAA regulations, I could no longer get lab results over the phone after his diagnosis. I even tried calling the Phlebotomy Department to see if they could look up his results and just tell me if he needed the appointment, but that wasn't an option either! The only way around it was to take Rick with me so he could personally get the report, and I would know whether to keep or cancel his appointment. Eventually, I provided a copy of his Power of Attorney to the hospital, which allowed me to pick up the lab report on my own. This routine went on for about four years!

Rick was such a brave patient and never complained about the procedures involved with his phlebotomy. He enjoyed chatting with the nurses and, of course, loved the part where we'd go out to eat afterward! Many times, he proudly told family and friends that he had asked the doctor what would happen if he didn't get the phlebotomies, and the doc had replied, "You'll die!"

We traveled to Las Vegas two days before Rick's 76th birthday and stayed at a Timeshare for the week. It was a much-needed break, though the June heat was intense. The day after we arrived—just before his birthday—he ended up in Urgent Care with a terrible rash on both arms that itched like crazy. Thankfully, the medicine they gave him worked wonders, and by the next day, his birthday was back on!

I had secretly packed birthday presents and decorations, and we celebrated from breakfast until bedtime. A "Happy Birthday" banner stretched across the room while he enjoyed breakfast, surrounded by festive presents. Our plan was to visit Wayne Newton's Casa De Shenandoah, but we missed the tour and had to make reservations for another day. Two days later, we returned bright and early for the amazing tour!

That little hiccup in our plans only stretched the celebration out longer. Without hesitation, we jumped in the car, and when we approached an In-N-Out Burger, the steering wheel automatically turned itself into the parking lot. After eating one of those infamous burgers with a few fries and a diet soda, we headed for our next destination.

For dessert, we found a bakery, picked up some cupcakes, and then walked off the calorie shopping at our favorite stores in the mall. Before we left, we even topped it all off with ice cream from DQ! You'd think we'd be stuffed by then, but a few hours later, there we were, enjoying a full-course dinner at Marie Callender's. It was a day of using no common sense when it came to food or calories! After all, it was Rick's birthday and our vacation!

Everything had gone smoothly until dinner, when I discreetly tried to hand Rick four pills to take. I placed them on his saucer, and he loudly announced that he needed to take them with food. "Yes, I know. I'm going to give you some cornbread," I said quietly. Since two family members had joined us, I think he felt confident in telling me with a raised voice that he wanted to handle it himself and, basically, to leave him alone. He made that very clear! It was the first time he had ever made a scene or spoken to me like that in public or at home. Needless to say, I was quite embarrassed and didn't want the situation to escalate, so I chose to say nothing at the time. But afterward, I made it clear I didn't ever want him speaking to me like that again.

The issue with his pills didn't end there. By the end of the week, I found some still in his pill box, meaning he hadn't taken all his medications. So, it was time for me to start monitoring his daily pills as well. Since I now kept all the meds in my room, he didn't object when I told him this would be the new routine. It was one less thing for him to worry about.

At that point, he wasn't paying as much attention to his clothes either. I assumed he was changing his underwear daily until I realized there were only four pairs in his hamper when I did laundry. He insisted he was putting on clean underwear every day, but there should have been seven pairs to wash! From then on, I made it a point to help him pick out clean clothes each morning and keep a closer eye on things.

Rick went for his yearly exam with the ophthalmologist, and it was recommended that he get his right eye "cleaned," just like he had done with his left eye in 2014. The membrane behind the eye can thicken over time, and a YAG Laser procedure would clean, or break, the capsule to allow more light to enter.

He was very excited with the results and said it felt like a light had been turned on, making his peripheral vision slightly more clear.

Afterward, he was able to somewhat look out of the side of his eye and catch glimpses of the scenery as we drove through town and down the highway. He also found it easier to watch our 56-inch curved-screen TV by turning his head slightly and looking out of the side of his eye. Unfortunately, this procedure did not restore the vision he lost in 2015.

Since his primary doctor had told him it was important to keep moving and not sit for hours at a time, Rick started walking on the treadmill at 1 mph. He began with just ten minutes and gradually increased his time to thirty minutes. His feet shuffled as he held on, and his head hung down, staring at his feet. He faithfully did this exercise for months, remembering that exercise could help keep his hemoglobin and hematocrit numbers down. His goal was to have as few phlebotomy appointments as possible. It became a bit of a game, and it gave him a sense of doing something proactive to improve his health.

Rick often mentioned to his eye doctors that he wished there were some kind of eye transplants available. At one point, I even called Utah Stem Cells to inquire if he might qualify for a procedure that could improve his eyesight, but I never heard back from them.

On good days, Rick could still pitch in and help like old times. He was great at plunging a clogged drain or trimming large branches off bushes with the pruners. Believe me, I really did appreciate the strength he still had in his arms and hands!

However, there were consequences if he overworked. One night, after helping out in the yard, he was awake at 1:15 a.m. with his neuropathy over the top, and even Lyrica wasn't helping. He walked the floor for about an hour before finally getting some relief from two Restless Leg Syndrome PM pills, which allowed him to get some sleep.

After I had washed and stemmed a double box of jumbo strawberries, I walked into the kitchen and found Rick popping berries into his mouth like candy—one of them was so big, it was practically a full serving! I couldn't believe my eyes. Years ago, he wouldn't have touched a strawberry, even if it was hidden in a bowl of chocolate ice cream. The same went for watermelon and cantaloupe, but once he reluctantly tried them, they didn't last long enough to spoil!

We were getting ready for a little trip around the July 4th holiday, and I had put an ice box in the car the night before. I mentioned to him that I wanted frozen ice gels added in the morning, but with his decline in comprehension, he didn't hear me correctly. The next morning, I discovered the warm, defrosted gels in the icebox!

We checked into our hotel, thinking we'd left all our problems behind at home. No such luck—they followed us! Whatever Rick had eaten during the day disagreed with his digestive system that night. One pair of underwear ended up in the trash while I cleaned the floor and carpet at the hotel. Being a caregiver doesn't stop when you're on vacation!

Back at home and time for lunch, I called out loud and clear that his sandwich was ready. A few minutes later, he brought KQ out and left him in the kitchen, then turned around and went back to his room. When he didn't return, I went to check on him and found him standing in front of his armoire, where the TV and computer were located. I returned to the kitchen and continued eating my lunch. Just as I was almost finished, Rick came back and commented on the food. I asked, "Didn't you hear me tell you your sandwich was ready?" He said he hadn't heard me, and I reminded him that he had brought KQ into the kitchen when I called him. His reply was, "I must have forgotten!"

Oh, some days I got so frustrated. It upset me when he didn't volunteer to do anything around the house. I would have to bring it up, like the poor bushes struggling on the side of the house in the middle of summer. He said they needed more water! Well, duh! So, I had to ask him to give them more water or add another drip line? He said he would do it, but it would be when he got good and ready. Another example was having to continually remind him to put the trash barrels out and ask him to bring them back in after the trash truck had emptied them.

Surprise, surprise! The next day, he woke up at six-thirty and had already installed another drip line by the time I got up at eight! He had also pulled weeds, but only the ones he could see! I made breakfast, but he had already eaten some strawberries. Like I mentioned earlier, they disappeared really fast! After breakfast, I hinted that he needed to take a shower. I guess he felt as hot and dirty as I knew he was, so he finally went in and took a shower. I thought he'd come out all clean and fresh, but to my dismay, he put his smelly, dirty clothes right back on! It made me feel like the Warden, constantly having to check and re-check everything, but that had become part of my role as a caregiver. He turned back around and changed into clean clothes afterward.

I turned the dishwasher on the night before when I went to bed, but when I entered the kitchen the next morning, Rick and KQ were already there watching TV. The green "finished" light wasn't on. I checked the dishes, and they were clean. I asked if he had opened the dishwasher because the light wasn't on, but he said, "No," that he hadn't touched it. Hmm. If he hadn't opened the door, the green light should have been on. Had it malfunctioned? Or had someone opened the door and just forgot?

After his phlebotomy appointment at the hospital one morning, they offered him some juice, as they always did after drawing blood. When they gave him a choice, he picked apple juice. Being a diabetic, eight ounces of apple juice spiked his blood sugar, but he wanted it anyway.

The night before, we had gone out to dinner. When the waitress asked what he'd like to drink, he confidently said to her, "I'll have an Arnold Palmer!" I had asked him so many times before to just order water at restaurants, since we had soda at home and didn't need the extra cost of drinks when we went out. But he didn't like water and would jump at any chance to drink something else if it was offered! I began to notice a pattern in his behavior when we were around other people. I sensed a bit of defiance or rebellion, which I feared could easily escalate into another scene like the one at Marie Callender's.

***

In July 2017, our little Yorke, KQ, had gotten very sick and was not responding to treatments by a local veterinarian. Out of desperation, I called another animal hospital and got him an appointment that same day. After X-rays and blood tests, which the first vet had not done, he was diagnosed with pancreatitis. With the right medications and lots of tender loving care, he recovered from this painful illness but was always more susceptible to upset stomachs.

Less than a year later, in May 2018, our 9 lb. 1 oz. KQ came down with his second bout of pancreatitis, and we almost lost him this time. Again, with the help of a dedicated veterinarian and lots of loving care at home, he gradually got better. There were many follow-up visits, with some good and some bad days. More bad days eventually overtook our little 8 lb. 3 oz. fur baby, and a chemistry panel disclosed that his sugar level was over five hundred! This new diagnosis of diabetes was heartbreaking, and we were left with the decision of whether to treat him or let nature take its course. I started giving him injections, but his little body cried in pain with every shot. After giving it a good try and several days later, I told him I wasn't going to torture him anymore. His little brown eyes looked at me as if to say, "Promise?"

We knew our time was limited. He had been our sweet fur baby for eleven and a half years. We prayed that he wouldn't suffer, although he had already endured so much. We asked God to give us guidance to do the right thing at the right time. Five weeks after KQ's diagnosis, he started having more frequent potty accidents in the house, and one night, he soaked the carpet. That's when I knew.

I told Rick that we needed to call the vet the next morning. On May 15, 2019, our 6 lb. 1 oz. KQ went to sleep while I held him on my lap. He was cremated and returned to us, with half of his ashes placed under a beautiful reddish-orange rose bush in our backyard.

***

Rick got new glasses after his yearly eye exam in July 2017, and the new frames were a good fit. However, the next morning, while looking out the window at a distance, he said his distant vision wasn't as clear as it had been with his old glasses. So, we had to return to LensCrafters. There was a significant difference— not just a slight change— when comparing his new prescription with the old one from the year before. The manager called the doctor's office, and it was discovered that a typo had occurred in the new prescription! It wasn't long before Rick was wearing another pair of new glasses, with frames he liked even better!

One day, Rick called his Masonic brother, Dick, and left a message about getting a ride to Lodge that night— but the meeting was actually the next night! Dick left a voicemail the next day while we were at the vet with

KQ, saying he'd pick Rick up at six o'clock. Unfortunately, Rick accidentally deleted the voicemail. When he took his cell phone outside to try and call Dick back, he inadvertently called my number twice. When I answered, Rick didn't realize he was talking to me, even after I told him. He still thought he was talking to Dick's wife! To make matters more confusing, Rick thought she had hung up on him. Then, Rick thought maybe he had called two wrong numbers, which he had. He was never able to figure out what had happened!

It was a very hot August, and I had already made at least three calls to the gutter company that had installed the gutters on our house shortly after we moved in. Finally, someone came out and finished installing a much-needed extension to the downspout in the backyard. While he was in the middle of that job, Rick went out to supervise—like he had been involved from the very beginning. "Once a boss, always a boss," I used to tell him.

A lot of times, I tried to overlook things, but when I was tired or overwhelmed, it was hard to get through some challenges without showing my frustration. During those moments, I looked to God and asked for His help. "This, Too, Shall Pass" was a constant reminder for me to move on!

Rick had been watching TV all afternoon after the gutter guy left. I had finished my treadmill walk and went into the kitchen around six-thirty to make dinner. Rick asked if he could use the treadmill, and I told him to go ahead, but he didn't leave the kitchen. Instead, he stood there until dinner was ready and then got himself a glass of water (yes, water!) —that was the extent of his help! After dinner, he took his dishes to the sink. He looked at the dishwasher, which had dirty dishes, and I saw him do something at the sink. I assumed he was getting ready to load the dishwasher. I put my dirty dishes on the counter and started putting things away in the fridge. When I turned around, I saw Rick standing by the pantry. I asked him what he was doing, and he said, "I don't know." I thought he had already loaded the dishwasher, but when I checked, all the dirty dishes were in the sink, not even rinsed. I asked him what he had done with the dishes, and as I started to load the dishwasher, all he could say was, "I thought…" I asked, "What did you think?" The conversation went nowhere. He went off to do his treadmill walk, and I continued cleaning the kitchen.

The next morning was just as confusing. Rick came into my bathroom around eleven-fifteen and asked if I was ready. I asked, "Ready for what?" It was a Wednesday, and we usually did some shopping for our friends, but we never left until one-fifteen. However, that week, we didn't have any shopping to do. I was leaving for a four-thirty appointment, and Rick had a Lodge meeting that night. So, he said he would go outside and fix the drip line, but it never happened because the temperature soared to 103 degrees.

When it was time for the Lodge meeting, Rick chose to wear his thin, white cotton, button-down Lodge shirt. When I saw how tight it was, I told him it wasn't a good choice. After some discussion, he said he'd talk to someone at the meeting and buy a new one. When he got home, he had brought someone else's cell phone with him after it had been left on a table. He told the person who drove him home that he'd make sure the phone got back to its owner. Rick wasn't in the condition to arrange this, but he took credit for being a good Samaritan! After that, it became very complicated for me with phone calls, giving directions, and getting the phone returned.

Rick knew this had taken a toll on me, and he asked if we could talk after dinner. As I've mentioned before, it was rare for him to initiate a talk. We both unloaded our frustrations, which was good to do once in a while! It made me feel like our marriage was normal again, like it was before Alzheimer's interfered.

A few days later, while eating dinner, Rick broke one of his molars down to the bone. After X-rays, an exam, having the tooth pulled, and a root canal, he agreed to a new implant. The implant was checked and rechecked, but wasn't healing according to plan. After six months into 2018, infection set in, and the bone had pulled loose from the implant, so it was going to be removed at the next visit.

Less than a week later, Rick took KQ outside after dinner. When he came back indoors, he said, "Look what I've got." As he held out his hand for me to see, I had no idea what I was looking at until he said with a grin, "My implant just fell out!"

A friend we had worked with in Palmdale passed away, so we made a road trip to California to attend his funeral. Rick took charge of the Garmin GPS as I drove into the heart of Orange County. There had been a few changes in the landmarks, but I relied on my instincts to quickly familiarize myself with the freeway signs, all while keeping up with traffic and avoiding any idiots who got in my way. At the same time, Rick started giving me directions, telling me to get in another lane. He yelled, saying I should have exited at the off-ramp I had just passed! Then he told me to get off at another exit, but I knew in my "mental map" that it wasn't the right one either. He even told me the speed limit was 75 mph, though I had just seen a sign saying it was 70 mph. I tried to stay calm and tune him out, focusing on my driving, and eventually, we reached the correct exit. By the time I navigated through traffic, found the hotel entrance, parked the car, and checked us in, I was a ball of nerves!

I told Rick I was taking him to a special restaurant for dinner, so he needed to freshen up and change his clothes. He resisted, saying he didn't think he needed to change. After he finally did, I made an excuse to stop by the lobby before we left.

Since Rick had worked in the El Segundo area before transferring to Palmdale, I secretly arranged a surprise meeting with two of his former co-workers at our hotel in Laguna Hills. Ted and John, two of his old colleagues, arrived as planned. As we entered the lobby at five o'clock, I spotted them sitting nearby, waiting for us. I smiled at them, and they nodded back as Rick headed straight for the candy dish at the counter!

I called out to Rick, but he was too focused on choosing a piece of candy. Eventually, he came over, chewing on his candy, and stood next to me without noticing who was right in front of him. I blamed his poor eyesight for not recognizing them, and after I introduced everyone, Rick was ecstatic once he realized who had come to see him! Ted drove us to Peppino's for dinner, and it turned into a memorable reunion for the four of us Boeing retirees.

The next morning, we attended the funeral of our friend and co-worker from Palmdale. It became another reunion for many of us who hadn't seen each other in a long time.

Afterward, we headed up the highway to Forest Lawn in Cypress to put flowers on his parents' graves. Driving through Los Angeles traffic that Saturday was a nightmare, but we made it safely to Lancaster to spend the night before heading home the next morning.

Once we were back home and unpacked, life returned to normal. Rick and KQ were already up and in the kitchen when I greeted them with, "Good morning!" The first thing I noticed was chocolate milk spilled all over the counter—Rick's second-favorite beverage those days. He had overfilled his glass during the night but hadn't made any attempt to clean it up, so I did that before breakfast.

The following day, Rick asked if he should take the sheets off the bed to be washed, and I said, "OK." When I later checked, I found everything, down to the mattress pad, piled up by the washer. There was blood on the mattress pad, sheets, and pillowcases— not just a little, but a lot! I pre-scrubbed everything with "Quick n Brite" before successfully washing everything.

After his Memory Class, I asked Rick where all the blood had come from, and he explained it was when he had dug those growths off his arm. A few days earlier, he had mentioned scratching them off, and I noticed a black spot on his arm, but I had no idea he'd done it while in bed or to such an extent. The dermatologist had recently removed a cancerous spot from his arm, so it probably wasn't a smart thing for him to have done!

We had good days, but it seemed like the bad days were becoming more frequent. Some days, we just needed to sit down and vent our frustrations. He had his, and I had mine. That part of our marriage wasn't new, and these talks helped. Most of the time, he made an effort to do better after these moments of realization. Sometimes, though, he tried so hard that he ended up getting in the way of what I was already doing!

There were days when I felt like I worked from the moment I entered the kitchen in the morning until the lights went out at night. Many days, the load felt too heavy, and there were not many offers to help. One evening, after dinner, I was clearing and rinsing the dishes to load into the dishwasher when Rick came to the sink and literally shoved me aside to rinse his own dishes. He didn't move afterward, staying at the sink while I was trying to continue what I had been doing. That was a perfect example of him doing what he wanted to do, but I would have much more appreciated it if he had done something that actually needed to be done rather than something I was already in the middle of!

I questioned myself afterward as to whether I should have just stepped aside and let Rick help in his own way. Maybe I should have appreciated anything he tried to do. Maybe I should have just thanked him for helping! I could question myself until I was blue in the face, but when I was in the moment, trying to get things done so I could move on to the next task, it was simply a matter of finishing one thing and moving on to the next on my list. He sometimes accused me of not appreciating him, and this topic often came up in our discussions. I used those opportunities to let him know what I did appreciate about him, giving examples of the jobs he had done and could still do that helped me. At that time, he was still able to help take care of KQ, open jars that I couldn't, have muscle power that I didn't, make his bed, fold his laundry, empty the trash, put napkins and silverware on the table, rub my back, and massage my feet. Small jobs, but meaningful things he could still do.

I also expressed many times how sorry I was that he was going through all these medical issues. I never wanted to see him in pain, and his pain became my pain. If he hurt, I hurt with him. I did my best to help, fix, or stop it—or, at the very least, give him a hug. All I could do was live in the moment, not let yesterday overtake today or worry too much about what tomorrow would bring. However, I was concerned about what the future might demand and whether I needed to prepare—or if I would be prepared. With those things, I had to trust in God.

Our doctor had told us that Rick's condition would get worse and eventually be more than I could handle. I often wondered, "What does 'worse' look like?" or "How bad will things get before I can't manage anymore?" Basically, what will “bad” be? We visited the VA Home in Southern Utah to inquire whether they might be an option if I could no longer care for Rick. They gave us an application to fill out, but it was filed away because I knew I could still take care of him at that point, and I didn’t think we were anywhere near that stage yet.

Some days, however, it already felt like things were getting worse. I found a paint can leaking all over a shelf in the garage, with three other cans stuck to it. I got three of them loose and asked Rick to get the last one unstuck, which he did. I then asked him to clean up the shelf. He responded that he was just going to cover the mess.

Later, when I checked again, he was looking in a toolbox. I asked, "What are you looking for?" He replied, "Something to scrape the rest off."

He explained that he had already scraped as much as he could and that the surface was smooth. A little while later, I found him looking in a drawer and asked again, "What are you looking for now?"

He answered, "Paint thinner!"

I told him we didn't have any and went back inside. When I entered the garage later and noticed two cans were back in the cupboard, a quick glance told me they were sitting on top of wet rags, or so I thought at the time! That evening, I asked him why he had put the cans on wet rags, and he insisted he hadn't. He claimed that none of the cans were leaking when he placed them on the garage floor and returned them to the shelf. This led to a disagreement. We both went to the garage, and I showed him the rags were soaked, not with water, but with paint. He finally threw away two of the cans along with the paint-soaked rags, but the incident still left me frustrated.

Other days, we would go around in circles, with me trying to get a message across and Rick trying to comprehend what I was saying. I had recently noticed he was beginning to repeat things I had just said.

As the holidays approached, we made our yearly trip to California to see our granddaughter perform as a Party Girl in *The Nutcracker.* After celebrating Christmas with our California family, we ventured to Las Vegas to spend Christmas Day with our grandson and more family. It was a holiday to remember, and there would never be another one quite like it.

After Christmas, we carefully packed all the decorations in the garage. The car was parked in the driveway, so Rick went into the house to get his car keys. I told him I would put the car in the garage, but he insisted he had done it before! I looked at him, thinking, "*Oh my gosh, when? When I wasn't looking?*" I reminded him that if something went wrong, the insurance wouldn't cover it since he no longer had a driver's license. That didn't sit well with him, and he was irritated at me for ruining his fun.

One day, he was pulling all the cards out of his wallet and organizing them, including a small stack of cut-up cards. While delivering laundry for him to fold, I peeked at the piles while he was in the backyard, and my jaw dropped—I discovered he had cut up two of his new 2018 membership cards!

We spent New Year's Eve at home, watching the clock move forward from East to West on TV. I made a plate of snacks for our cozy twosome as fireworks flashed on the screen. When it was time to turn out the lights and say goodbye to 2017, Rick asked if he could get me anything. The day was over, the year was ending, and it was time to say, "Good night."

CHAPTER 05 | Hopeful Horizons

The year 2018 started out with us switching to some new doctors. Rick's eye care was transferred to a large eye center nearby, where all his appointments could be consolidated under one roof. We were also dealing with his tooth implant through March, as previously mentioned. A new dentist came on board in August! On top of that, Rick's phlebotomy, cardiology, podiatry, dermatology, chiropractic appointments, and Memory Matters classes continued to fill our calendar.

In January, Rick began a series of twenty Hyperbaric treatments in the hope that they would relieve his neuropathy and help his Parkinson's. We were also hopeful that it could miraculously improve his brain function. He was desperate to try anything that might improve his quality of life. He was always optimistic and the perfect patient, smiling, at least on the outside! While we didn't see any significant outward changes, he said his neuropathy wasn't as painful, though that feeling changed from day to day. There wasn't a magical change, but we were hopeful he would be better after completing all twenty treatments than he was before starting them.

Looking back, we're glad we tried—better than just wishing we had.

We continued to stay as active as possible with social events—going to block parties, Bunco, Bingo, movies, plays, concerts, Elks, Masonic events, eating out, visiting friends, and attending church as often as possible. It was important to stay involved to maintain a positive outlook and focus on living life to the fullest.

I started noticing that Rick was slurring his words more when he tried to explain something. His voice would trail off as he spoke, making it harder for me to understand him. A conversation came up about when he graduated from high school, and he couldn't remember the year. A card had been mailed to one of his daughters, and when I asked if he knew her birthday, he couldn't remember that either! As time went on, he became more confused and struggled to comprehend simple things I would tell him—like rinsing a dish before putting it in the dishwasher. Instead, he stood at the sink, scrubbing it. One time, he asked if he should throw away a baggie full of dishwasher pods or "soap," to be more specific!

During a Memory Matters class, Rick got up about twenty minutes before I arrived to pick him up. The leader asked where he was going, and he said he was leaving because I was there. The leader later told me that he had seen a lady with the same hair color as mine, though hers was messy. In the past, he had never mistaken someone else for me—at least, not that I was aware of!

That same night, he stood in front of the TV with the guide showing on the screen and the remote in his hand. It didn't seem like he knew what he was doing, so I asked if he was searching for a particular news station. With that question, he snapped to attention and said, "What channel?"

He also began changing clothes frequently, sometimes up to three outfits a day! There was always a reason—sometimes justified, sometimes not. He preferred to wear a freshly ironed shirt and rarely wanted to wear one that had been hung up after being worn just once.

We had a statue of a little boy with a fishing pole sitting on the ledge outside a front window. I had painted his hat blue to match the flower pots in the yard. When I was finished with my artistic paint project, I told Rick to come outside and look at the hat. His comment was not what I expected! He said, "The hat's just the right size!"

I attended an all-day course in St. George on Dementia Dialogues, sponsored by the Five County Association of Governments. This program was offered by the Office for the Study of Aging and the South Carolina Department of Health and Human Services. It covered five separate topics: (1) The Basic Facts: An Introduction to Dementia, (2) Keeping the Dialogue Going: Communication Skills, (3) Preparing the Environment: Safety, Activities of Daily Living (ADLs), and Quality of Life (QOL), (4) It's Nothing Personal: Addressing Challenging Behavior, and (5) Now What Do I Do? Creative Problem Solving.

During one of the discussions, they asked if I had any idea what my plans would be after this journey was over. Without much thought, I blurted out that I thought I might write a book! To my amazement, they encouraged me and said they would love to read it if I did. At the end of this very informative day, I received a Dementia Specialist certificate after successfully completing all five sessions of Dementia Dialogues.

Having completed the course, you might think it would have made my job easier as a caregiver. However, no one can predict what challenges lie ahead. One day doesn't necessarily predict the next. We caregivers are always on standby, ready to address the unexpected at a moment's notice. As human beings, we sometimes have to make rapid decisions without time to think them through.

This class gave me valuable information and was a helpful tool to guide me through the rest of my journey with Rick. However, it didn't prepare me for all the challenges that were yet to come.

We also started taking a new over-the-counter supplement—grape-seed extract—from the health food store. It seemed to give us more energy. One morning, I found him already up, dressed, and heading outside as I came into the kitchen. He said he was going to replace some sprinkler heads but hadn't eaten breakfast or fed KQ, which he might or might not do on any given day! Seeing me, he came back inside to eat breakfast before heading out again. What began as a simple task of replacing sprinkler heads turned into a bigger project of digging up old lines and replacing them with new ones. He wanted to do it right! Given his limited eyesight, the task was more difficult than he had anticipated, and it continued into the next day.

The following morning, Rick was already working in the backyard when I went outside. He was in the middle of his sprinkler job when I noticed he was wearing one of his newer white pullover shirts with a pocket and his good New Balance shoes. This was definitely an "Oh My Gosh" moment when I saw the condition of his shirt.

I asked, "Don't you have old white shoes for the yard?"

Silence.

After a pause, he came up with an answer, "Those old white ones hurt my feet!"

Of course, I didn't buy that story. They say you should pick your battles, but people who say that probably haven't walked in the shoes of a caregiver! For me, every day could bring at least one "battle," if you want to call it that. It takes patience, understanding, and a lot of willpower to remain silent in many cases.

As for the dirty white shirt, I treated it with Quick n Brite before washing it, and it came out looking like new! As for the shoes, we could always buy another new pair.

It can be hard to keep quiet when you know the conversation is completely off course. Often, you need to weigh the pros and cons before taking action. It isn't always an easy decision to make in the moment, but a caregiver—much like a parent—is forced to make the right choice at the right time and do the best they can. We, as caregivers, need to remember that we're not perfect either. A day can bring many unpredictable scenarios, and hindsight is always 20/20. If you keep dwelling on things when you close your eyes at night, you'll never be able to turn your brain off and get any rest.

One of the beautiful things about being together on this journey is that it's never too late to say, "I'm sorry," while hugs and "I love yous" can be exchanged anytime the urge hits. This journey as a caregiver is a real education.

As Easter approached, we colored and decorated eggs. Rick completed four eggs and decided he was done halfway through the fifth. When he was done, he was done and just walked away!

A few days earlier, we had talked about stopping our lawn service and using that money to help pay for his Memory Matters classes. He asked how much the classes cost, and when I told him, he seemed surprised. He didn't think we should have to pay anything and wanted to know if others had to pay as well. I said, "Of course, do you think they only make you pay?" He just shook his head.

His next idea was to visit the bookstore to find a Bible with a large print. I led the way to the religious section, thinking he wanted one to read at home. When he stopped at the customer service desk to ask if they had large-print Bibles, I decided he didn't need me there and wandered to another section. After a while, I moseyed over and found him sitting on the floor looking at Bibles on the bottom shelf. He knew which version he wanted, so that narrowed down the options. I asked if he'd found what he was looking for, and he said, "No!" He wanted a Bible with large enough print to read at church, but I didn't think he'd be able to keep up with the pastor and recommended against it. We left empty-handed, as there were no Bibles with large enough print for him to read. That frustrated him!

From the bookstore, we headed to the nursery to buy more sprinkler heads but ended up coming home with a new lawn mower! I had planned to mow the lawn, but Rick informed me he was going to do it himself. I told him I didn't want him stumbling into the mower, and he said he didn't plan to. He even joked for me to be on standby in case he needed to go to the ER! He managed to do a little mowing, but not much.

One day, before a doctor's appointment, we were ready to eat lunch when Rick came out of the bedroom holding a can of beer. I assumed it was an empty can he wanted to throw away, but it wasn't. He took a drink, and I asked why he was drinking a beer before going to the doctor. He held up the can and said, "It's not beer." I pointed out it was the brand he always buys, and he looked at the can in surprise. "Oh, I thought it was a Sprite Zero!" Now, I knew his eyesight wasn't great, but trying to convince me he couldn't taste the difference was another story I wasn't buying!

He could easily find himself in the doghouse—and I don't mean KQ's! To make up for it, he decided to wash the windows while I was gone. I didn't want him falling off any ladders, so he washed off the patio and side yard until I got home. Nice job! Then, with me supervising, he climbed the small step ladder to wash the windows. He was proud of his work and kept complimenting himself throughout dinner. I couldn't resist throwing in a few compliments for the delicious dinner I had prepared, too!

The next day, after breakfast and a haircut, he returned to finish the windows. When it was time for lunch, he came in, and I asked if he'd washed his hands. "No," he said—something I often had to remind him to do. After lunch, he went back outside and gave the windows their final shine. When he finished, I suggested he take a shower and shave. His response? "It's done!"

He was walking on the treadmill as much as possible, at 1 mph, for 15 minutes twice a day. Since his Hyperbaric treatments, he seemed more motivated to improve his health. He even got back on the computer and found a website with instructions on how to tie a tie. He had forgotten how several years ago and wanted to master it again. He kept practicing until he managed to tie it correctly once, but he couldn't repeat it after that.

The doctor had Rick check his blood sugar three times a week. Since we were preparing to leave for California, I told him to get his test kit from my bathroom, where I now kept all the meds. We each had our own cases—his was black, and mine was blue. He completed his test and told me the number, but when I went to record it in his logbook, I discovered he had used my monitor by mistake, throwing off my average!

While he was at a Memory Matters class, I baked some chocolate chip cookies. When we got home, Rick said the house smelled good. I asked him what it smelled like, and he said, "Chocolate rolls." So, I gave him two cookies!

We attended church a few days later, and Rick asked me how old he was going to be on his next birthday. Knowing he would be seventy-seven and surprised he had even asked, I told him eighty-five! Then I asked, "How old are you now?" He replied, "Eighty-four!" At least he could still do some math!

For my birthday, we became kids again and went to Disneyland for two days. We walked much slower and at the same pace we used to see older people moving when we were younger! Sitting more often gave us the opportunity to people-watch, rest our tired feet, and dodge thousands of strollers! Of course, we also did our fair share of eating, with lunch at the V8 Café, dinner at the Pacific Wharf Café, and a glass of wine at Mendocino Terrace. Once we felt ready, we rode "Soarin' Around the World," "Radiator Springs Racers," and "Toy Story Mania" in California Adventure. The next day took us to the old, original Disneyland, where we started in the "Tiki Room," then ventured over to the scenic "Railroad" tour, found the "Monorail," drove the "Autopia Cars," strolled down the river on "Mark Twain's Riverboat," sailed on the "Columbia," rode through "It's a Small World," and ended the day by watching the Pixar Parade. The day wouldn't have been complete without eating at our favorite "Blue Bayou" restaurant!

As we traveled back home on I-15, with me at the wheel going about 79 mph, Rick shifted positions in the passenger seat. I suddenly heard a "pop," and the car began losing momentum. Just as I realized he had accidentally knocked the gear into neutral, he quickly shifted it back into drive and then, again, into neutral! I tried to accelerate, but nothing happened because he couldn't see what he was doing. He wasn't driving anymore, and after this, he was officially fired as a back-seat driver! If he couldn't be in the passenger seat or back seat, where do you think his next place would be to ride?

Since Rick had once loved painting pictures with watercolors, I thought he might enjoy painting again and give him something constructive to do. We went to the local big-box store and bought a package of stretched canvases, a variety of acrylic paints, and a little plastic palette. He didn't like the palette and said he'd never used one like that before, but I put it in the basket anyway, just in case this adventure went somewhere. He also needed a new twenty-four-inch stool, so we picked that up, too.

As we were leaving the store, Rick noticed some fresh flowers on display for Mother's Day. To my surprise, he picked out a beautiful bouquet and said he wanted to buy it for me! It had been rare lately for him to buy me flowers like he used to, so I really appreciated it and loved seeing that old spark come to life again.

We rearranged his bedroom for the fifth time in two years to accommodate his paint easel and the new supplies. He was enthusiastic at the time but never touched the paints. After several months had passed, I quietly packed everything away, and he never seemed to miss them.

When we pulled out the dresser drawers to rearrange the room, I discovered one of his red shirts wadded up among his pajamas. I also found a brand-new, unopened colored ink cartridge for his printer that had expired four years earlier!

The St. George Masonic Lodge sponsored a Books for Bikes contest for elementary students who read the most books during the school year. A bike, helmet, shirt, and certificate were presented to one student in each grade at several different schools, and Rick was honored to be one of the presenters that year at the school nearest our home.

He mowed the lawn with our new electric mower after I inserted the battery and key to get it started. He then walked around the mower, just looking at it, and I asked what he was looking at. He got mad and told me to leave him alone! I watched as he struggled to put the catcher on—it was hard for him to see where it hooked. He needed help but eventually managed to do it on his own. Mowing the edge of the lawn was difficult due to his eyesight. It wasn't his best lawn mowing job, but it was the best he could do at that time.

During a violent windstorm, one of our baby ash trees snapped in half, and Rick decided he would dig it out and replace it with a new one. About a week later, he complained that he didn't feel right. I asked if he thought he should get checked out, and he suggested a visit to the chiropractor might help. He also mentioned that his eyes weren't focusing as they should. The chiropractor adjusted his hips and lower back and advised him to be very careful with them! Digging out that tree and planting a new one had taken a toll on his body.

The next day, Rick took a long nap and woke up very dizzy and unable to move his feet. He sat on the edge of the bed for a while before he could walk, but he remained dizzy for some time.

He had his yearly eye exam a few days later, and everything looked normal for what his "normal" was, except for the middle of his left eye. His left eye was the only one in which he had some vision left, and it didn't look very healthy at this appointment.

We purchased cemetery plots many years ago but had never selected headstones, and it seemed the delay weighed on Rick's mind. He started hinting that we needed to pick out our headstones, and I could sense a certain urgency in his voice that I couldn't quite place. So, I made an appointment.

We decided on a double headstone instead of two individual ones, and Rick seemed overly anxious to make decisions for his half. Without hesitation, he quickly spoke up, detailing exactly what he wanted: a Past Worshipful Master's emblem and a United States Air Force Veteran's medallion, which would come from the Veteran's Administration after his passing.

Once Rick was satisfied with his choices, it was my turn. The whole process was computerized, and we saw and approved the design before leaving. After the business was done, I could sense a kind of peace coming over Rick. The monument company advised us that the headstone would be placed at the cemetery as soon as it was completed because they couldn't store it.

Weeks later, we were notified that the headstone had been installed on our plots. It felt surreal to see our names and birth dates set in stone while we were both still alive and standing there. Yet, it also felt good to have that business taken care of. Rick's biggest concern, as he looked at his half of the headstone, was, "Where is my Veteran's medallion?"

A couple of weeks later, Rick got up early to mow the lawn since we were expecting company that day. It started to rain just as he began, but he kept on pushing. I thought he would come in out of the rain, but he didn't seem to notice how wet everything was getting. I told him I didn't want the mower to get wet and risk any issues, so he quit in a huff and didn't have much to say to me for the rest of the day.

Our company came, and his personality changed completely! You would have thought he didn't have any medical problems as he visited and chatted, sounding as if he had it all together. He sure fooled our guests—one of them even commented, "He seems to be doing really well!" I knew some of what Rick said was fabricated, but our company didn't know any different. After they left, Rick took a nap while I cleaned. When he woke up, he went out and finished mowing the lawn and still didn't have much to say to me.

Rick's blurred vision continued to worsen, but he still puttered around the yard doing tasks that seemed a little beyond his ability at that point. We had baby trees that needed constant attention after strong winds either snapped them, whipped the branches, or blew one particular tree into a horizontal position on the ground that awaited our help for survival. Rick climbed a six-foot ladder to pull the tree upright. Between the two of us, we managed to save it, securing it back to the stakes that should have held it in the first place. But as he carefully stepped down from the ladder, he missed the bottom rung and landed flat on his back. I had been standing nearby to prevent an accident, but it happened too fast for me to help. Thankfully, he didn't hit his head, and both he and the tree survived.

When he tried to re-stake another tree before the wind could destroy it, he struggled to figure out how to thread the wire through the stake's hole to go in one direction while the second wire went the opposite way. He couldn't see the hole, but he was determined to do it himself. He became so frustrated that I knew when not to open my mouth and offer help, so I stepped away. When he finally gave up and asked for my help, we did it together.

I placed a happy face sticker over the 30-second button on the microwave so he could see it easily. However, when I used the microwave later, I discovered the sticker had been switched to the six-minute button! Thankfully, it was me pressing it this time, or the smoke alarms may have gone off.

While driving down Interstate 15, Rick remarked on how empty an RV park looked as we passed it. I hadn't noticed, but on our way back, I looked more closely and saw it was actually full. Was his eyesight really that bad, or were his glasses just dirty?

I thought Rick was behind me as we headed to the checkout line at Costco, but when I turned around, he was nowhere to be seen. I asked if the store could page him, but they didn't have a paging system. I checked out, took the groceries to the car, and then went back inside to search the entire store.

Eventually, I found him heading toward the exit. Where had he been? Why, he had stopped for free samples at the food booths!

While I was watching TV one evening, Rick came in and asked if the things in the washing machine were clean. I had no idea what he was talking about and told him I had just put two dirty towels in to be washed later. He responded, "But the sign says they're clean." It turned out he was actually talking about the dishwasher, not the washing machine! This miscommunication was common—his brain knew what he wanted to say, but different words came out of his mouth.

On a Thursday morning, we were headed to his Memory Matters class when I realized he hadn't shaved. Despite my reminders, he had skipped both a shave and a shower for two days, and now he was on his third without shaving. His color choices for outfits were also becoming a problem, with mismatched or wrinkled clothes that looked like they had come straight from the hamper. Once upon a time, he would only have worn a freshly ironed shirt! This happened again at his dermatology appointment, and I realized I would need to start inspecting him before we left the house.

One night, while he dozed in his chair holding a glass of Cactus Cooler, the drink slipped from his hand and hit the floor, spilling everywhere. He slowly got up and went to the kitchen to grab some paper towels and tried to clean it up, but his efforts only created more work for me to clean the floor that remained sticky.

His vision was clearly declining. He looked at his pill case one day with a puzzled look and asked if it was his. When I assured him it was, he insisted it didn't look like his usual orange one. Recently, he came indoors after being outside and sat down in his chair. He said his Levis looked purple, and his turquoise shirt appeared green. He could still distinguish reds and greens correctly, but his eyesight was definitely playing tricks on him.

We stopped to buy groceries after church one Sunday morning, and Rick helped unload the car when we got home. Once he was done, he poured himself some chocolate milk and grabbed a handful of nuts. When I offered him a sandwich, he eagerly accepted. I finished my lunch and left the room, but when I came back, he had fallen asleep at the table, still holding his half-eaten sandwich!

One of his daughters texted us a bunch of pictures, so I handed him my phone to view them. I showed him how to scroll and enlarge the images, assuming he understood. When I returned, he was still engrossed in the phone, but somehow, he had wandered into the wrong text thread and had sent a series of random emojis to one of my friends! When I showed him where he was compared to where he should have been, he acted as if he didn't know what I was talking about.

That same friend and I tried to meet for lunch once a month. She and her husband had been our friends for many years. A few days later, Rick and I attended the local Heritage Choir's Flag Day concert, and I mentioned that I should have invited them to join us. Rick's response was unexpected: "I don't get invited to her luncheons!" I had to explain to little Ricky that our lunches were a "girl thing." Truth be told, he didn't really like me going out to lunch without him!

Rick's health continued to decline. Standing at the kitchen sink, looking out at our newly installed patio cover, he tried to explain something to me, but his words were so slurred that I had no idea what he was trying to say. His mother had also suffered from

Parkinson's, and seeing Rick at this stage brought back memories of her journey.

After an ultrasound was performed on his left foot due to pain between his second and third toes, Rick was diagnosed with Neuroma, which is caused by a pinched nerve and repeated bruising from walking. He received a cortisone injection and was given a fifty-fifty chance that it would help reduce the pain.

After a month, Rick returned to the foot doctor for a recheck. As he waited for the doctor to come in, he sat rubbing his right foot. The assistant asked him about the percentage of improvement since his injection, and he chuckled because he wasn't sure.

She suggested, "Maybe seventy-five percent?" and he replied, "Yes."

I chimed in, pointing out that it was his left foot we were discussing since he was still rubbing his right foot. The assistant confirmed it was indeed his left foot, and Rick quickly switched to rubbing the correct one. I added that I thought his foot was a lot better because he hadn't been complaining of any pain. The assistant asked if it felt better than seventy-five percent, and Rick agreed that it did.

We celebrated his seventy-seventh birthday in Mesquite, Nevada. It was less than an hour's drive from home, a fun getaway for some gambling, and a good restaurant where we enjoyed a delicious salmon dinner. We both did well and came home winners!

One morning, I noticed he was more confused than usual. After breakfast, he unloaded the dishwasher one item at a time and then loaded it with the dirty dishes. Yes, he still insisted on doing things his way! Later, he watched some TV and dragged his feet through fifteen noisy minutes on the treadmill. Those walks were more difficult when it became harder to lift his feet.

I reminded him what time we needed to leave for his dental appointment and what he needed to do before we left. He took his shower, made the bed, and had some of his clothes on when I checked back in. But he seemed to be looking around aimlessly, not sure what he was looking for, just going in circles. I left him for a while, and when I returned, he was sound asleep on his bed.

He sat up when he heard me come in. I asked how he was feeling, and he said his eyes were blurry.

"How does your body feel?" I asked.

After a moment's hesitation, he said he needed to take deep breaths. I asked if he thought he needed to go to the ER, and he said no—but I told him I'd be the one to decide that later! He seemed to be dragging with less energy, which concerned me.

I questioned him again, trying to get more specific answers: "Do you feel weak, tired, have no energy, or have a stomachache?" He responded that he was just tired and wanted to sleep.

At his next dental appointment, they discovered an abscessed wisdom tooth that needed to come out. Rick thought he could avoid having it extracted, but I reminded him that he didn't want the infection to spread to his brain. Maybe the infection was also why he hadn't been feeling well. That explanation seemed to satisfy him, and he agreed to the extraction.

The tooth was pulled without complications. I made him two poached eggs when we got home, but even eating those was difficult for him. The next morning, he woke up dizzy, and the following days were rough. His lip and the inside corner of his mouth were sore, his right eye hurt, and his jaw was painful. There was some swelling, but it wasn't too bad.

By the third day, he felt well enough to go shopping with me and to have lunch at Golden Corral. He managed to find some food he could eat, but during lunch, he knocked over his glass of iced tea, making a big mess. This was the second time recently that he had knocked over a drink at the table.

About two weeks later, Rick stumbled into the doggy gate while heading into the kitchen. The gate hit the trash can, tipping it over, and Rick ended up on top of the pile! He said he was okay, but his right arm and elbow were bruised. He took a long nap that afternoon, and I kept a close eye on him.

He had also fallen asleep in the car after I picked him up from a Memory Matters class. He had painted a piece of art during class, and as we were getting ready to leave, his instructor asked where it was. He told her he had trashed it! She seemed surprised to hear that coming from Rick, but that kind of response was not uncommon, considering the students that were in her class.

When we got home and pulled into the garage, Rick murmured something like "Home…" I got out of the car, and as he opened his door, I unlocked the house to let KQ out. But when I turned back, Rick was still sitting in the car. I thought he was just changing his glasses, but he had fallen asleep! As I stood by his door, he woke up, got out, and staggered. He was disoriented, so I took his arm to help him walk into the house.

***

Our grandson Walt was graduating from the Marine Corps Recruit Depot (MCRD) in San Diego, California. This was an event we had been planning to attend for months and did not want to miss. Our hotel reservations were at an ancient hotel in Old Town, within walking distance of shopping and restaurants. We drove to the Bayside Inn at MCRD late that afternoon for the "Meet the DJ's Social" and met up with other family members who had also traveled to San Diego for the graduation.

Rick and I took off on foot that night from the hotel to have dinner, and that's when we realized it was too long a walk for him. As he put one foot in front of the other, the only thing that kept him going was knowing there was food at the other end! Café Coyote, by far, had the best Mexican food this side of the border! After that long, tiresome walk back to the hotel, future trips were by car! Rick managed to push through that first day, but he was exhausted by the time his head hit the pillow that night.

Family Day started at eight-thirty the following morning. There was a long security check line at the gate, where everyone had to exit their vehicles and leave everything inside except their identifications. The car hoods, trunks, and all doors were left open for the sniff dogs! Everyone had a body scan done, then stood at a different location until notified to return to their vehicles.

Once inside the facility, there was a lot of walking ahead of us. We met at the Depot to watch the recruits doing their run and afterwards drove to the theater to hear what being a Marine was all about. By that time, the new Marines were returning to their barracks to shower and change into their dress uniforms. From there, we headed back to Bayside Inn for lunch, where Walt met us! After lunch, it was free time, so we walked to the mall inside MCRD.

Graduation followed the next day, and we got another early start, leaving the hotel at six-fifteen. By leaving that early, we were one of the first in line for the security check and then proceeded to the Admiral's Quarters to hear the Marine Band, introductions, etc. Then we walked to the parade site and took our reserved seats in the grandstands to cheer for the four hundred seventy-seven new graduates, especially one!

All the activities and lots of walking took a toll on Rick. At one point, as we walked through the old historic Depot, it became clear that he was beginning to drag his feet more. Despite all the precautions I took to avoid any mishaps, there was always one that got overlooked or unheard. With uneven walkways and steps in the old Depot, I reminded him that we were coming to a step, and it only took one time when he didn't raise his foot high enough. He hit the ground with a thud. His son Jess witnessed the fall, as did other family members, and immediately helped his dad get back up. Rick admitted afterward that he needed to use his cane, but no one could have convinced him before the fall. It had to be his idea!

As Rick became more exhausted, signs of confusion started to show. At one point, he mixed up the names of his son and grandson, and even asked if his son was also a Marine! It was clear that all the activity had worn him out, but despite the challenges, we were grateful to have been there to support Walt on such a significant occasion.

CHAPTER 06 | Sudden Twist

After being back home for a week, Rick was feeling ill and took a couple of days to recover before dental, eye, and infusion appointments resumed.

We were on our way to another Memory Matters class, and the garage door wouldn't close using the remote. I asked him to get out and close the door using the wireless entry box, but I wasn't sure if he'd be able to see the keypad well enough to do that. Instead, he went inside the garage, closed the door, and opened it again. He came back out, got into the car, and told me it worked and was fixed! I got out of the car, closed it with the keypad, and replaced the worn-out batteries in the remote when I got home.

One day, I had gone to get my nails done and needed to take him for his lab test when I got home. There was no specific time to be there, but I told him I'd be ready to leave about thirty minutes later. Since there had been severe weather the night before and I hadn't gotten much sleep, I told Rick I needed to lie down for about ten minutes before we left, and we could get something to eat afterward.

I asked if he had fed KQ while I was gone, and he said he had been sleeping. He wanted to get on the treadmill and do his exercises before going for his blood test, and he said there was no hurry to get to the lab. That surprised me since he was always ready to go if it meant we were going to eat out.

Then, when I went into the kitchen to feed the dog, I discovered jelly smeared all over the counter. It looked like the finger painting I did when I was in the second grade, and it irritated me that he didn't clean up after himself. I went in and asked him if he had eaten anything while I was gone, and he said, "No." My irritation turned up a notch, so I told him what I had discovered all over the counter. He looked bewildered and then remembered that he had eaten a peanut butter and jelly sandwich! It wasn't so much the mess I had to clean up that upset me; it was him not telling the truth when I asked. He said he had forgotten! Okay, did he really forget he had eaten a sandwich while I was gone? He said he had been sleeping. Why didn't he feed the dog while he was eating? Days like that just wore me out.

About three days later, he looked more tired than usual and seemed to be hunched over more when he walked. He was making careless decisions, like putting an empty milk carton in the freezer, placing dirty dishes in the clean dishwasher, and later emptying both the clean and dirty dishes from the dishwasher. I asked if he was feeling okay, and he said he was feeling a bit puny and that his eyes weren't focusing well. Later, I went outside to pull weeds from around the sprinkler heads in the lawn. He came out, asked what I was doing, and made the comment that it would've been easier to whack them off with the weed eater. As an expert, that's what he would have done!

New issues seemed to pop up every day, and it was clear that Rick was becoming more clingy. He would appear unexpectedly behind me or beside me, wanting to know what I was doing. Sometimes, he would wander into my bedroom while I was folding clothes or making the bed, just wondering where I was.

He had a new partial plate made after his wisdom tooth was pulled. After losing that tooth, a total of four teeth were missing, and he didn't feel like he could chew on that side anymore. It was a real effort for him to wear the partial, and I took him back for adjustments at least four times. Eventually, he threw the partial plate in a drawer and never wore it again. With no dental insurance, it was just another expense gone to waste!

Then he got a notion after watching something on TV about cornea transplants and thought maybe he could get his eye fixed and start driving again! I told him DMV would have to approve it first, and he said that would be no problem! When he asked the doctor about that possibility, he was sadly reminded that it was his retina that was destroyed, not the cornea, and he felt defeated once again.

Thanksgiving was quickly approaching, and he asked me what day it came on. I said, "It comes on the same day every year. What day do you think it comes on?" He replied, "Saturday."

Since one of his Lodge brothers was picking him up for a meeting that night, I told him he needed a haircut beforehand. As he was sitting on the stool getting his haircut, along with all the extras he would get from a professional, he couldn't stay awake! I suggested he lie down afterwards and take a nap before he needed to leave, and that's what he did.

Thanksgiving Thursday finally arrived, and our grandson, his wife, and our two great-granddaughters drove up from Las Vegas to spend the day with us. We were stuffed with turkey and all the trimmings by the time we left the Golden Corral that afternoon, and even better, it was my day off from cooking!

Rick used to always put Christmas decorations up in the yard every year after Thanksgiving. This year was no exception, and he proudly set four small decorative trees out in the yard. When it came time to connect all the trees with extension cords, he couldn't figure out the right sequence in order for them to turn on together. Something that had always been a no-brainer was now a puzzle. We got that job done together, and then he was ready to bring a big Santa Claus out of storage to continue decorating! He proudly added lights to the trees and bushes in the yard. His collection of decorations would not have been complete without a three-piece train where the locomotive looked as if it was in motion when its lights came on. A few years before, our decorations had been chosen as the best-animated yard in the neighborhood!

St. George is notorious for celebrating the holidays that bring tourists in from all the surrounding states. We were always two locals who were among the thousands in town to visit the Dickens Festival and the Jubilee of Trees. In addition to those celebrations, we also attended the Southwest Symphony Orchestra and the Heritage Choir for their big Christmas concerts. Christmas was a very special time of year for both of us, not only for its true meaning but because we also celebrated our wedding anniversary in December.

Our annual California trip was upon us once again to visit our two granddaughters, their mom, stepdad, and Debbie for a holiday visit. One of our granddaughters had taken ballet since she was four years old, and this would be her ninth performance in The Nutcracker. We arrived two nights before the ballet and met our grandchildren and their parents at a local restaurant for dinner. Afterwards, we headed back to the hotel to exchange Christmas gifts. With their busy schedules, this was the only time of year we could see them.

We took a short drive from Santa Clarita to Palmdale on the morning of the performance and visited two close friends we had worked with at Rockwell International (now Boeing) before we moved to Florida. It was a beautiful, sunny day traveling through Bouquet Canyon into the Antelope Valley, where Palmdale is located.

Debbie arrived at the hotel that evening before we all left for MiMi's Restaurant. Then off we went to The Nutcracker for a spectacular performance! Afterwards, the three of us stopped at Denny's for light refreshments, and Rick chose to eat a big hot fudge sundae!

***

Sunday morning, December 16th, we were planning to check out of the hotel and head north to visit one of Rick's daughters and her family. I got up first and showered before Rick was awake, then eventually went in and told him he needed to get up and get ready so we could go down and eat breakfast before checking out of the hotel. I assumed he heard me, although he made no effort to get up while I stood there.

While I was in the bathroom drying my hair, I heard a loud bang and assumed it was the neighbor's door slamming shut as they left their room. Typical hotel noises when everyone is checking out on a weekend morning! Shortly thereafter, I went back to check on Rick and didn't find him in the bed, nor did I see him anywhere at first. Then I heard a groan and found him on the floor between the bed and the wall, maybe a sixteen-inch space, with his head up in the corner facing down. Half-joking, I said, "What did you do, fall out of bed?" All I heard was a groan, another, and another. Then I knew this was no joke, and immediately knelt down and said, "I'll get you out of there. You push, and I'll pull." More groans. I grabbed his ankles and started to pull, but one foot was lodged under the bed frame. I gently gave it a little twist, and it popped free. By the grace of God, I pulled him out of the corner to the foot of the bed.

As soon as he was at the foot of the bed and out of that corner, he sat up in a slouched position and said in a very slow, slurred voice, "I don't know what happened." As soon as I saw him trying to talk, I knew he had suffered a stroke! Immediately, I ran to the house phone to call for help, but there was no dial tone. I pressed one button after the other and got nothing. The phone was out of order!

I told Rick to just sit there, and I was going for help. I opened the door and ran to the elevator, dodging a family coming down the hall, pulling all their suitcases. I heard the lady say, "Let her go first." As I entered the elevator, I pressed the button for the first floor. I reached the front desk and desperately blurted out that my husband had fallen and I needed help! They said they would send someone right up. I turned around, caught the elevator, and was back beside Rick in a jiffy. Before anyone arrived, I took Rick's blood sugar because that was all I could do at the time. It was acceptable. I asked him questions such as, "What is your name?" "Who is the President of the United States?" He gave me answers, but I wasn't sure what he said because of his mumbling.

Then I heard a knock on the door. I yelled to come in, and there stood a young man, or maybe an older boy, with no clue as to what to do! I realized immediately that I should have told them at the desk to call 9-1-1, but I wasn't even thinking clearly at that time. So, I told the kid that Rick needed paramedics! He took off in a flash, and we waited for what seemed like forever. I didn't know if he had told the desk to call 9-1-1, so I told Rick again that I was going downstairs and not to move! I repeated the same trip to the elevator as before, still dodging more people who were checking out.

As I approached the desk, the paramedics and fire trucks were just arriving and coming inside. The first fireman greeted someone at the desk and shouted, "Find out who owns those cars outside the front door and tell them to move their cars NOW! That zone is for emergency vehicles only." Another paramedic met me, and we headed to the elevator. On the way up, I gave him a recap of what had happened and told him I was sure Rick was having a stroke.

Soon, there were at least four paramedics checking Rick, but he had crawled to the bathroom by the time we returned and was unable to get up. After a quick evaluation and finding his blood pressure was 190/110, they quickly had him on a gurney and wheeled him downstairs to a waiting ambulance.

By the time I had canceled our checkout with the hotel and received assurance for an extended stay, made some phone calls, and arrived at the hospital, they had given Rick a blood clot-busting med. They were still in the process of doing an X-ray and CAT scan. He was soon diagnosed with a 9mm stroke in the left thalamic area of his brain that affected the entire right side of his body and his speech.

Debbie wasted no time in arriving at the hospital after receiving my phone call. She stayed with me all day, giving much-needed support in the first hours of this unexpected, life-changing event.

While he was in the hospital, he complained that his right ankle hurt, so they X-rayed it. They advised me that an orthopedic doctor had also been called on board in addition to the neurologist. They were taking precautions with his ankle until that doctor had a chance to review the X-rays and visit us at his bedside. To our surprise, his ankle had a spiral fracture! They chose to have him wear a boot instead of a cast when he was out of bed. What compounded the problem was that his right arm, hand, leg, and foot were almost useless at that point. His speech started to return three to four days later and eventually improved enough for him to be understood. Already battling Parkinson's, recovery from the stroke would be a challenge. The fractured ankle compounded his recovery even more!

My thoughts went back to when I pulled him out from between the bed and the wall. Had I fractured his ankle when I gave the ankle a twist to unlodge his foot from under the bed? The thought haunted me that I might have added injury to injury, but the orthopedist assured me that I could not have done that kind of fracture to his ankle. So, it remains a mystery as to how his foot managed to get lodged and cause a spiral fracture. He had no memory of the fall, paramedics, or the ride in the ambulance! I know in hindsight that he fell when I thought the neighbors had slammed their door shut!

He spent three days in the hospital before being transferred to their Acute Rehab Unit. It wasn't an automatic move from one hospital building to another. Our medical insurance was advised by the hospital that Rick's condition was critical enough that they did not recommend he be moved to any other facility. There were other facilities in the area, but the hospital's Acute Rehab Unit was known to be the finest. We kept our fingers crossed that our insurance would give their approval.

After authorization was received for Rick to be admitted to the Rehab Unit at the hospital, he was transferred late Wednesday night after his stroke on Sunday morning. As a new rehab patient, he had a complete evaluation and physical exam upon arrival.

Once he was settled into his private room and in the hands of experts, I drove back to Utah two days later to get things in order. I picked KQ up from the kennel when I got home, made new reservations for him to return for an extended stay, unpacked suitcases, made an inventory of what Rick might need in the hospital, shopped for items he didn't have, and repacked our suitcases.

His three daughters had all come to the hospital to visit their dad. After the two younger daughters had returned to their respective homes, the oldest daughter, Donna, stayed at the hotel and spent every day with him while I was gone. She oversaw all of his therapy sessions, shopped for items she felt he needed, interacted with the staff on his behalf, kept detailed notes of all doctor visits and activities for me, and decorated his room for Christmas! I drove back to California on Christmas Eve day, while she had flown home earlier that same morning to spend Christmas with her family.

Rick's room was right next to a small dining room, and the staff was at a minimum on Christmas day. The two of us spent that very quiet Christmas together in a cheerfully decorated room where he opened a few presents, and then I wheeled him into the dining room, where we enjoyed our Christmas dinner that was provided by the hospital. At this stage of his recovery, he needed help doing everything. He was not able to feed himself, and swallowing was accomplished very carefully.

His physical and occupational rehabs were vigorous and extensive in this hospital facility, and I was advised that his recovery could take up to a year or more. In addition, they advised me that his chances of having a second stroke were much higher after having this first one. Rick's Parkinson's, dementia, low vision, and fractured ankle all slowed his progress even more. It was their plan to discharge him on December 29th, once he was stable enough to travel.

The hospital staff ordered a wheelchair specifically to meet his needs. The first one delivered was not equipped with the accessories they asked for, so it was sent back;

but the second wheelchair arrived and met with their approval.

Donna and her husband, Dave, flew back to California on December 28th to give us the support we desperately needed. I knew I was in no position to drive Rick back to Utah by myself, and it was frightening to think of what it would take physically to help him with any needs along the way. With Dave's EMT training and ER experience, he and Donna were the angels we needed! Rick had the utmost confidence in Dave, so that was also a bonus.

However, before Rick could be released, the three of us were required to have a mandatory safety course on how to transfer him from the wheelchair to the car and back to his wheelchair. We thought this short course would be easy, but it was a huge effort since Rick's right side didn't cooperate very well. Even with a transfer belt that we purchased, it was no easy task!

In the meantime, the hospital staff was limited between Christmas and New Year's, but they were persistent in trying to get proper signatures from the Rehab Facility in St. George so that Rick could make a smooth transfer from one facility to another. Unfortunately, authorization did not come through in time for Rick to be admitted when we arrived in St. George. So, we ended up taking him home and were totally unprepared!

When we left the hospital early that Saturday morning, Rick was sitting in the passenger seat next to me, just like he did two weeks before when we had arrived in California. Only this time, Dave and Donna were following us in their rental car. First, we had to stop at an out-of-the-way pharmacy that was open twenty-four hours a day to fill several prescriptions. Pharmacies close by were not open, nor was the hospital pharmacy at that early hour! After another hour had passed and prescriptions were filled, we were on the road for home.

Instead of taking six or seven hours to drive from California to Utah, it took ten hours because of the pharmacy stop and holiday traffic. The first rest stop was beyond crowded, and the handicapped restrooms were occupied by others, with people waiting in line to use them. Dave took charge and maneuvered Rick up and out of the car. He held the door open so that Rick was hidden from onlookers. While Donna and I stood facing the outside to complete the enclosure, Dave helped Rick do his business in a urinal!

When we stopped to eat at a restaurant, Dave helped Rick with all the transfers to and from the wheelchair and the restroom as well. Everything went well that time!

We drove directly home and arrived that night after dark. The Christmas decorations were all lit up in the front yard just as Rick had left them, as if to say, "Welcome home!"

One of the first things that needed to be done was to move furniture to accommodate Rick's wheelchair. The bathroom was not equipped for the handicapped until Dave made a trip to Home Depot the following day and installed a toilet-support rail, grab bar, and a transfer bench for the shower. Donna assisted Dave and me whenever we asked, and she was a big help even when she wasn't asked.

They both left to take a short break one evening. Rick was sitting on the couch watching TV when they left, and it appeared everything was under control. As soon as they were out the door, Rick said he had to go to the bathroom! I thought, "Oh, no!" Now, it was my turn to transfer him from the couch to the wheelchair, which I had not done on my own. Rick knew what he was supposed to do, and I knew what I had to do, but working as a team wasn't working very well. He didn't have the confidence in me like he did with Dave, and I didn't blame him! I also didn't have the strength to lift him the way Dave did.

I was trying to stay calm while he was becoming frustrated and trying to tell me what to do and how to do it. I almost got on the phone to call the kids back home, but we finally worked together and got through that first panic!

We had hoped the phone would ring with the news that approval had been received for Rick to be admitted to the local rehab facility. Sunday was our twenty-ninth wedding anniversary, Monday was the last day of the year, and Tuesday was New Year's Day. The phone did not ring, and it was a long weekend!

***

The four of us ate lunch at the Olive Garden on Wednesday of the new year, still waiting for the phone call to admit Rick to the rehab facility. It was refreshing to start the new year with optimism that 2019 would be better than how 2018 had ended.

Just as we were preparing to leave the restaurant, the phone rang with the call we had been waiting for! Since Dave and Donna had reservations to fly back to Oregon and were planning to leave that afternoon, I knew that God was in charge, as He always is. This was no coincidence! We didn't know what His plan was, but His timing was perfect!

Rick was admitted to the rehab facility on January 2nd to continue his physical and occupational therapies for his right side. He was somewhat of a difficult patient, as his dementia made it hard for him to remember what he had been told, and it was difficult for him to carry out instructions.

An orthopedic doctor came on board shortly after Rick was admitted. His ankle was X-rayed and showed that it was healing nicely, but he was to continue wearing the boot. A follow-up visit later that month confirmed the bone had healed, but calcium was still forming. He was given permission to wear a shoe indoors, but he had to continue wearing the boot outside for two more weeks.

He had his own wheelchair at the new facility, but one day, a tear was discovered in the seat. I notified Medicare and was transferred to a local representative. Arrangements were made to get a replacement, but it didn't happen without communication problems!

I arrived for one-of-many visits the evening of the fifth, just after he had slipped off the bed. Of course, there wasn't time to put the boot on before he landed on the floor! It was his first fall after the stroke, and it seemed like his body had gently folded to the floor as he slipped off the bed. He was lucky to have not done any further damage to his ankle.

I received a phone call at six-forty the next morning, reporting his fall the night before. The nurse who called seemed surprised to learn that I already knew! She had no idea that I had arrived as they were picking him up and putting him back to bed.

Rick told me that he hadn't received his pills until eleven o'clock the night before. All I could do was ask questions, but there wasn't much I could do if I wasn't there. At least they knew I would speak up on Rick's behalf, and they were aware I was in and out a lot while he was a patient. Another factor I had to consider was whether Rick had his facts straight!

Insurance became an issue when they only approved Rick to be in rehab for two weeks. So, he was discharged on January 16th and put on Home Care, with an RN, a physical therapist, and an occupational therapist coming to our home until the end of February.

***

On February 4th, he woke up and tried to get dressed. When I entered the room, he was very disoriented and didn't know where he was. He asked me how he got there and wanted to know if I had brought him. When he seemed to be completely awake, he said he had had a dream where someone had driven him to our house and told him to go inside and get dressed. He thought he had to go to the bathroom and pointed to the other side of his bed, where he thought he had gone. I checked that side of the bed, and the floor was wet, as well as the bedding and the side of his mattress.

The following day, we started the first of twelve laser treatments on his ankle with another doctor. This was to generate more calcium and promote healing. X-rays taken the following month by the orthopedic doctor showed more healing had taken place, so his physical therapy could start soon. Laser treatments were not covered by our insurance, but we chose this as an elective to expedite his recovery.

On February 6th, the RN came for one of her evaluations. The three of us were in the kitchen, and she was showing me something on her phone. When Rick decided he also wanted to see, he got up from the stool he was sitting on and forgot that he couldn't stand on his right leg. He lost his balance and tumbled into the refrigerator, but the noise was worse than the fall. She and I helped him up, and he didn't appear to be injured. After the RN left, I went to Walmart to get some groceries and pick up a prescription for him.

He was sitting in his chair watching TV before I left, and I reminded him to stay there while I was gone. He promised to do just that! When I returned, I knew something was amiss when I saw his walker in the kitchen all by itself. As I looked into the living room, he was standing in front of the couch, moving his right arm around. I asked him what he was doing, and he said he had fallen. His right shoulder was very painful, so I told him to stop moving it and sit down! We were expecting his physical therapist to arrive later, but the doorbell rang a half hour before she was due. That was no coincidence; the Good Lord had sent her early!

It upset me that he had fallen and was hurt after promising he would not move from his chair while I was gone. I had groceries to bring in from the car and put in the refrigerator or freezer. While shopping at Walmart, my phone rang about an issue with his wheelchair. After that call ended, I continued my shopping and headed for the checkout. Once home, I realized I had forgotten to pick up his prescription!

The physical therapist immediately took charge, trying to determine what his injuries were while I put the groceries away. She called the RN, and we all agreed that he needed to go to the ER. She immobilized his shoulder with dish towels and helped him into the car. She followed us to the hospital and helped him into a wheelchair upon arrival. X-rays were taken of his arm, ribs, and chest. He also had blood work, an EKG, and two CAT scans. Everything looked normal, but by eleven-fifteen that night, they decided to admit him overnight for pain management. The ER doctor told me he had discussed the CAT scans with another doctor, and one showed a blockage in an artery at the back of the head leading to the neck, but it was not a factor in the fall.

Rick later admitted that he had gone to the kitchen to get a snack while I was gone. His walker tipped over when it got caught on something, and he fell over the walker onto his shoulder and arm. Then he crawled to the living room! Seeing him fall or knowing he had fallen and watching him suffer with pain absolutely tore at my heartstrings.

When I arrived at the hospital the next day, Rick was walking down the hall using his walker, accompanied by a physical therapist. The therapist thought he was doing great and discharged him to go home on February 7th.

On February 13th, the first of twelve laser treatments were started on his shoulder, in addition to the ones he was already receiving for his ankle. On February 15th, he had a gentle chiropractor adjustment to his upper back, neck, and shoulder areas. He also received an ultrasound and E-stim (electronic stimulation) on his shoulder.

I noticed the little lamp in his bedroom was unplugged, with the key that turned it on and off sitting next to it on the dresser. My first thought was that he had unscrewed it while trying to turn the lamp on, but when I tried screwing it back in, the entire bulb mechanism came loose! All attempts to re-seat the bulb failed. So, I called Rick in to help. He denied doing anything to the lamp and said he would fix it. Unfortunately, it turned out the lamp was beyond help!

It was a disaster when Rick tried to navigate his urinal in bed! Without going into all the details, I'll just say I was doing laundry at two o'clock in the morning on several occasions. Something needed to change, but I wasn't sure what or how! Was it time for Depends? I had already bought him some, just in case! When I opened the package and pulled one out, he wanted to know what he was supposed to do with it. He asked if he was supposed to pee in it and then put on a new one. We definitely had some work to do in that department!

He woke up one morning complaining that his arms and legs were asleep but couldn't really describe the symptoms. He was to have a laser treatment later that day, so they turned the laser energy down for his shoulder. Afterwards, he said it didn't hurt anymore, but the pain never completely went away. Then it returned with a vengeance, and he described it as being in his entire body. No over-the-counter remedies could relieve the pain, nor could any prescription.

He was checked out by his primary physician and got some adjustments to his medications. The cardiologist was pleased with his lab numbers, and phlebotomy resumed at the hospital for his Polycythemia.

On March 1st, Rick had a follow-up orthopedic visit for his broken ankle, which was improving nicely. While there, Rick told the physician's assistant (PA) how much pain his shoulder had been giving him. An MRI was ordered due to the constant pain and his limited range of motion. In the meantime, he was sent to the Health Performance Center to have them evaluate the shoulder. Their test showed Rick's shoulder wasn't frozen, but they suspected a rotator cuff problem.

The MRI of the shoulder on March 14th revealed two torn tendons, one of which was the bicep that would require surgery to repair.

He also had a routine dental appointment for X-rays and a cleaning on March 22nd. During the exam, a lesion was discovered on the side of his tongue, so he was referred to an oral surgeon. Surgery to remove a cluster of white spots from his tongue was performed on April 1st, and a biopsy was sent to the University of Utah in Salt Lake City. Thankfully, the results came back showing it was only a virus!

A week after his oral surgery, Rick had rotator cuff surgery as an outpatient. Donna came back again for her dad's surgery and kept her ears open at night for any sounds of pain since her bedroom was the closest to his. He received a pain block that was supposed to keep the area numb for hours after we got back home, but it didn't work, and the pain he suffered was over the top. I made calls to the doctor, and he was prescribed pain medication for the severe tear repair he had just gone through.

The next several days were difficult with pain management and trying to find a comfortable place for him to sleep. I tried making a bed for him in his leather chair with a footstool and plenty of pillows. The next morning, the stool was upside down and a distance away from his chair! He went in for a post-op appointment a week later after experiencing blood oozing from the incision. Once the surgical tape was removed and the incision cleaned up, the PA said everything looked good.

April 21st was Easter Sunday. Rick took a nap on his bed and was sleeping somewhat better now. When he got up from his nap, he walked to the TV located at the foot of his bed. It's unclear why, but he lost his balance and fell directly into the TV and the small table it sat on. Of course, the side that hit was the newly repaired shoulder! By now, the doctor had given me his personal cell number, so I was able to reach him immediately. He told me to bring Rick into the office the next morning.

An X-ray of the shoulder didn't show any break, but the doctor was secretly keeping his fingers crossed that no damage had occurred. Rick started physical therapy for the shoulder while therapy for his stroke was put on hold. Our calendar was jam-packed with appointments, and that seemed to be the norm nowadays.

When May rolled around, I took Rick to InstaCare because his ears were plugged again. This was a job only a professional could tackle, and it was never an easy task for them to remove all the wax buildup.

Then, it seemed like Rick was doing and saying off-the-wall things that left me scratching my head. He came out of the bathroom pushing his walker but was having trouble. It didn't seem to want to move, and then I noticed he was pushing it backwards!

He came into the office and asked me where we had been watching TV the night before as he pointed out the window toward our neighbor's house. He knew it was in a room, but he didn't know where. He thought and pointed, saying, "It was towards that way!"

One evening, I told him to get his pajamas on. He got his walker, walked to the hallway, stopped, and asked me what he was supposed to do.

I saw him looking under his chair, so I asked, "What's wrong?" He said, "The flashlight was right there," as he pointed to the end table, "and now it's gone." I got on my hands and knees, looking under the chair and the end table. There was nothing there, but I did find it on top of the coffee table where I should have looked in the first place!

On May 7th, the wind was blowing like crazy. I looked out my bedroom window just in time to see another one of our baby ash trees split in half and hit the ground! I announced the news to Rick as I dashed through the living room and out the sliding glass door. Unbeknownst to me, Rick got up from the couch to follow me but lost his balance on the wooden floor and went down right in front of the TV. He was just trying to get himself up when I came back inside. As usual, he hit his right shoulder and was in a lot of pain afterwards.

After another bad night, I called his orthopedic doctor the next day and took Rick in to be examined. The diagnosis was Costochondritis, an inflammation of the cartilage that connects a rib to the breastbone. As explained to me, it was a separation of cartilage and ribs.

CHAPTER 07 | Trespassers Emerge

The following day, he seemed to be suffering from spasms when he woke up from a nap. He couldn't get up and called for me to help. He said it had also happened during the night. His right arm and hand hurt, and it felt like his leg was swollen. I gave him a Mirapex pill and applied ice, but I ended up taking him to the ER later that day because his pain was so severe. After an X-ray, they discovered he had a broken rib from the fall two days before.

A few days later, he slept in his chair in the living room. There was a pillow and blanket on the loveseat, and he pointed at it and said someone had been hiding under the covers. He also pointed outside and said there were more rocks on the hill behind our house!

This was our conversation at dinner one evening during that same time period:

He asked, "Are these people from the railroad who have been here?"

"What people? Have there been people here?"

"Yes, they've been here."

"No, there hasn't been anyone here today. Have you seen somebody?"

He kind of laughed and said, "There have been three or four here!" Jokingly, I said, "Oh, they're probably Angels from Heaven!"

Very seriously, he said, "There's been an older lady sitting there" (he pointed to the kitchen table) "and a younger one sitting over there" (pointing to his living room chair).

I asked, "What are they saying?" He replied, "I don't know."

"Do you recognize them?" He said, "No."

I had a single white hydrangea in a vase on the coffee table, and he wanted to know who THAT was!

It was two in the morning when he entered my bedroom with his walker. I asked what was going on, and he said he didn't know where he was and that he had never been in this room before! I got up to see that every light in the house was on except one. He was very confused about why everything had been moved around and asked why I was doing this to him. I took his blood pressure and checked his sugar; both were fine. As this continued, I made him some hot chocolate and got him settled back in his chair to sleep. He told me to go back to bed, saying I didn't need to sit there and watch him!

At seven that same morning, we got up and were eating breakfast by seven-thirty. While eating, he kept looking out toward the backyard and asked why THEY were holding "stage" curtains up on our windows. I tried to convince him there was no one there, just the two of us. He said he didn't know what was happening to his eyes, so I cleaned his glasses.

Later that morning, I heard him talking while I was in another room. Thinking he was talking to me, I went in and found him "talking to all the people sitting in the living room." He was irritated that they just looked at him and turned away! He eventually went into his bedroom, sat in his rocking chair with his feet elevated, and watched TV. He said he felt safe in there!

I didn't know what was behind this behavior at the time. Maybe it was caused by his stroke, maybe all the pills he was taking, maybe Parkinson's, maybe Alzheimer's, or all of the above. Adding these hallucinations to his list of medical conditions was a big adjustment I wasn't prepared to face. I never knew from day to day, minute to minute, what to expect. I felt like I was sitting on a time bomb, waiting for it to go off!

In addition to keeping the two of us afloat, I was also taking care of our sick Yorkie, Kurly Q. As I wrote earlier, he had been diagnosed with diabetes after suffering two episodes of pancreatitis. During this time, we made our last trip to the veterinarian. We were escorted to a quiet, peaceful room with soft lighting, where Kurly was prepared for his final sleep. Rick was on his knees beside me as I held KQ, rubbing his ears as he took his last breath. We held his little lifeless body for quite some time before drying our eyes and leaving with heavy hearts.

I thought Rick had taken the loss of KQ better than I expected, but I was a basket case for several months. Weeks passed, and one night, Rick went to bed but suddenly appeared back in the doorway and just stood there. I asked him what he needed, and he didn't say anything before all the emotions he had held inside came gushing out in big sobs. All he said was, "I miss Kurly!" It was one of those moments when I instinctively jumped up and wrapped my arms around him. He cried until he had no tears left, and then he went back to bed.

On one of our outings, I was helping him get ready and reminded him to use deodorant and brush his teeth. After he picked up the deodorant stick, he rubbed it all over his stomach!

We went grocery shopping together, which was a bit of a challenge to have him keep up and not get lost in an aisle. However, this time, he drove an electric cart! With his low vision and learning how to operate the cart, I wasn't sure how safe it would be for the other shoppers, but there was only one way to find out! After a few lessons on how to stop and go, steering the cart was a no-brainer. No one got hit, and he had the greatest time driving this new toy! It was the first of many more driving adventures.

After Rick had completed nineteen physical therapy treatments for his shoulder, it was now the first of July. All stroke therapies had been temporarily discontinued until the shoulder healed, so now neuro sessions were going to resume.

However, when Rick showed up for his post-op visit, the orthopedic doctor was not happy with his shoulder progress. The doctor felt Rick should have had better movement in the shoulder by that time but hoped further therapy with his neuro sessions might help. He wanted to keep a close eye on the shoulder and scheduled yet another post-op appointment. Instead of Rick improving with all the therapies, his pain level climbed even higher!

He and I discussed the "what ifs" and whether a second MRI might be needed. The constant pain in his shoulder had become unbearable, even after continuing his neuro therapies, and he said he just wanted it fixed! During one of these sessions, he had another fall.

A second MRI was scheduled for September 13th, and the news was not good. The rotator cuff surgery was completely destroyed, as well as new areas of the shoulder, and the shoulder would not hold up for another surgery. In addition, a third tendon was also torn!

***

On October 15th, Rick underwent surgery for a complete reverse shoulder replacement and spent four days in the hospital. Donna returned once again to be with her dad and helped wherever she was needed, but she had to return home three days later. He came home with a pain "block" that worked this time, but he had a headache that wouldn't quit. His Home-Care RN, PA, and physical and occupational therapists were all scheduled to start the following day, including weekends. His shoulder bled during the night, so the PA removed the bandage and discovered Rick had several skin tears from the surgical tape. A close eye was also kept on the pain drip to prevent any complications.

On October 24th, he had a spell where the pain in his head and neck was very intense. He described the pain level as a twenty! When I put breakfast on the table, he was unable to hold a spoon, so I spoon-fed him, and he was able to eat a little. When he got up from the table, he just stood there, but his feet wouldn't move. His attempts were unsuccessful, so I told him to sit back down. He got up again, but his feet still wouldn't move. I asked, "Isn't your brain telling your feet what to do?" Finally, one foot barely moved, and then the other followed, maybe an inch. I helped him with his walker, though it was still difficult for him to put one foot in front of the other. He was very unsteady, and his right foot was turned out.

The RN came to the house, and the PA from the orthopedic office instructed her to draw blood and take it to the lab. The next day, I took Rick to another post-op shoulder appointment. During this visit, we used his wheelchair. All the lab reports from the day before looked fine, and a new prescription was given for some edema. They didn't feel the headaches were related to the surgery, but if they persisted over the weekend, I was told to take him to the ER.

On Saturday, October 26th, his headache was no better. I wanted to take him to the ER that night instead of letting him go to bed. When I was buttoning his shirt so we could leave, he shoved me away and said he wasn't going! I didn't pursue it further and let him go to bed.

He woke up Sunday morning still with a headache, but this time, he described it as only an eight. I fixed his breakfast, but he only ate a little yogurt. I knew I had to convince him to go to the ER, so I told him that if he stayed home, I was afraid he was going to die. I guess the big "D" word was powerful enough to get him thinking because he agreed to go. We were in the ER by eight-thirty.

After being examined and undergoing several tests, he was admitted to the Neuro Medical Unit for five days. An MRI confirmed that he had suffered a frontal-lobe stroke, and all the progress he had made from his first stroke was now history. Many other tests were performed during those five days, and the Neuro team was confident he was stable enough to begin rehab again.

It was Halloween when Rick was transferred to a rehab facility. He had a private room, similar to a fancy hotel, that included a remote-controlled leather recliner. While the staff got him settled and took his vitals, I sat in the recliner. I was a little apprehensive about him being left on his own, especially at night. They had no idea how his Alzheimer's, low vision, and strokes interacted.

The next day, I arrived to find that he had survived the night and was all smiles when I walked into his room. When I sat in his leather chair, I noticed the entire left side was broken away from the chair. Rick claimed it was that way when he arrived, but I had sat in the chair the day before, and it wasn't broken then. I was sure Rick had fallen asleep in the chair the previous night and, being disoriented upon waking, had come out fighting like Hercules. Without question, the staff replaced his chair that same day!

Rick wanted me to eat lunch with him every day, so I made reservations to meet him in the beautiful dining room at noon. Sometimes, we were entertained by volunteer pianists, and sometimes, we sat at a table with other patients. One such patient was Jim, whose wife Jolene sometimes joined us for lunch. Jim and Rick became good friends and ate other meals together when we, the wives, weren't there.

Rick spent four weeks there receiving extensive therapy for his new shoulder, aggressive therapy for walking, and non-stop therapy to help regain the use of his right side. It was nearly impossible for him to use his right hand, so he sometimes compensated by using his left, but he couldn't write with either hand.

He was discharged the day after Thanksgiving, not necessarily because he had improved that much but because the insurance company decided it was time to go home. Jolene and I stayed in touch after Rick left, and our friendship continued even after Jim went home. With both of us becoming long-term caregivers during Rick and Jim's journeys, she and I remain close friends to this day.

Rick's new shoulder didn't have the pain the old one had caused him, and he was very encouraged during his post-op visits. Everything was going well in that area. Two weeks after his discharge from rehab, he was allowed to lift up to two pounds with that arm!

He started physical and occupational therapies as an outpatient at the hospital, which included trying to get his hand to work again. He mentioned to the OT that he had once been an engineer and had been able to write and draw with that hand. Looking somewhat discouraged, he said, "Look at my scribbling now."

It was a bit of a challenge to bring him home from rehab and figure out what he was capable of doing on his own and where he needed help. He was able to walk slowly by using his walker.

He thought he could shower by holding the showerhead in his left hand, so I helped him get set up on the shower bench with the curtain closed. At one point, the shower curtain and rod ended up on the floor!

We had moved to our current home over three years earlier, and out of the blue, Rick asked, “How do we share our time between this house and the other one?” When I told him we had sold the other house, he said he didn’t know.

I was working out in the backyard a few days before Christmas while he slept inside. When he woke up, he opened the sliding door and asked if I had a cat in the house—but we didn’t own one!

Later that day, he complimented me on how nice the front yard looked. I told him I hadn’t been in the front yard, only the back. He said, “Oh, I thought I saw you in the front!”

Since it was the end of 2019, I felt it was a good time to have Rick’s cell phone turned off since he was no longer able to figure out how to use it.

He had not attended Memory Matters since his first stroke in 2018, but I was thankful for the two years he had been able to participate in their activities. It had been something he looked forward to once a week, but after the stroke, he didn't seem to remember that it had been the one outing he had always enjoyed on Thursdays!

***

We welcomed 2020 with hopes that things would settle down. I always tried to stay positive at the start of each year and felt relieved when the old year came to a close. I loved new beginnings, knowing that when one door closed, another would open. I looked forward to those new doors, though they weren't always what I hoped they would be.

Rick continued all of his outpatient therapies through January and resumed his monthly lab visits and phlebotomy appointments for his Polycythemia. Eye appointments with the retina specialist also continued for examinations of both eyes, along with injections in his left eye.

January, however, didn't pass without incident. On the last day, Rick had his first fall of the year. His foot missed the transition from grass to the cement walkway, and he fell hard on his right shoulder! He stayed on the ground for at least five minutes before trying to get up. His arm, hand, and right leg hurt, and his elbow was skinned. The following week, an X-ray of his shoulder showed no dislocation or break, but it remained quite sore, and it took three to four weeks for him to recover.

In mid-February, Rick was approved to receive Palliative Care at home for two months. A physical therapist completed an assessment and determined he would not need nursing care but would benefit from additional physical therapy.

The following week, he lost his balance in the garage while getting out of the car and fell backward into an empty trash barrel, causing a second empty barrel to fall on top of him. Thankfully, he wasn't hurt this time and was able to get himself up by using his walker.

At the end of February, my only sister passed away unexpectedly. The news hit me harder than I could have anticipated, and my emotions hit rock-bottom. As much as Rick had declined, he slowly got up and wrapped his arms around me. I will always remember that moment of love and tenderness he was able to give when I needed it the most.

As we prepared for a trip to California to attend my sister's funeral, Rick gathered up his things while I did the same. When it came time for him to pack his suitcase, I supervised and made a few adjustments. Most of his selections were fine, but he seemed particularly focused on taking four belts! With a little help, he was ready to go.

This trip was a bit easier than the one to San Diego, as Rick spent more time sitting and didn't get as tired. He gave me the moral support I needed, and I was grateful he could be there for me.

With the outbreak of Covid-19, we left California just hours before the state essentially shut down. Many businesses temporarily closed, and some never reopened. People were urged to stay indoors, and masks became a requirement outside. The virus spread worldwide, with each state implementing its own mandates. Once we were home, we isolated ourselves and stayed indoors. I only went grocery shopping when absolutely necessary and left early in the morning to avoid crowds.

Other than the medical staff visiting Rick, we discouraged all other visitors. Rick was especially worried about catching the virus due to his other medical conditions and made it clear to me that no one else was invited to visit.

When the two months of Palliative Care were up for renewal, the RN contacted our primary care physician for approval. Instead of continuing that care, the doctor said he believed Rick qualified for Hospice. This news hit me like a lightning bolt, and I had no idea how Rick would react to hearing the word "Hospice." I wasn't sure if he would actually comprehend the gravity of that care. If he did, would it send him to an early demise? I chose not to tell him why his care level was changing and instead explained that more help would be coming. That simple explanation seemed to satisfy him.

However, it was a challenge to keep the word "Hospice" from being mentioned when some of the medical help came. Certain individuals used it freely in their conversations, while I cringed every time I heard it, fearing that Rick would grasp its meaning. If he really comprehended what they were saying, he never batted an eye.

The Hospice RN arrived for an evaluation, and Medicare approved the care for six months, with reevaluations every two months thereafter. We had more traffic coming in and out of the house, with an aide assisting Rick with showers a couple of times a week, along with visits from a chaplain and social worker. Rick didn't mind the aide's help; she was quick and efficient.

Rick woke up feeling dizzy for a couple of days. Sometimes, he felt better after breakfast, sometimes not. The RN suspected dehydration and encouraged him to drink plenty of water. He seemed to feel better when he did, but water was never his favorite drink, and it was a struggle to get him to drink it, even when it was right beside him.

He saw a little girl come into his bedroom one evening and kneel beside his bed as if hiding. He said "Hello" to her, but she didn't respond.

That same morning, he said he saw someone standing on the hill behind our house, looking into our yard. I knew he couldn't see that far, so I chalked it up to another hallucination. With the frequent uninvited "guests" he was seeing, I would just make small talk and offer general comments, which seemed to temporarily satisfy him.

The dizziness continued to come and go. In May, Rick said he had been dizzy at two o'clock when he got up that morning to use the bathroom. He claimed he had to hold onto the wall to keep from falling, but this didn't make sense with his walker being right next to his bed. His stories weren't consistent, and it was harder for me to know what to believe.

He also had a different kind of episode in May. He took a nap before dinner and seemed to be in a deep sleep, but he woke up to eat. Afterwards, he sat in his chair in the living room and fell back into a deep sleep. Around 9:20 p.m., he suddenly woke up with a combative expression, his body rigid and his hands clenched tightly. He slouched in his chair, pushing against the back with his feet outstretched, touching the floor. He passed some "air" and was moaning. Then, he fully woke up and struggled to sit upright in his chair. Immediately, he looked at the TV, smiled, and waved to someone he believed was inside the screen!

It reminded me of the broken arm incident in the recliner at the rehab facility—same scenario, I think!

I witnessed this strange episode while sitting in the chair next to him, but he never acknowledged my presence. The next morning, I asked him about it, but he had no memory of it happening.

***

Three days later, Rick was in his bedroom and fell when one foot stepped on the other! Another version I heard was that his shoe caused his foot to twist. He caught himself on the arm of the recliner, but his chest took the brunt of the impact. That night, he complained of chest pain, and sure enough, there was bruising! It was thought that his pain pills were contributing to his dizziness, so their use was reduced.

Going out to eat was one of the rare pleasures we still had, and after one of his eye appointments, we went to Chuck-a-Rama for lunch. Many restaurants were either closed, had shorter hours, or offered limited menus due to Covid. When Rick returned to our booth with his plate carefully placed on his walker seat, he stumbled, causing his plate to slide onto the booth seat, and his food ended up on the floor!

A few days later, he started complaining of neck pain. He went for a long-overdue chiropractic adjustment and had an ultrasound on his neck and shoulders, but the pain didn't seem to improve, and he needed a pain pill. When that didn't work, the Hospice RN arranged for a muscle-relaxer prescription to be delivered to the house. Even with that, he woke up at 2:30 a.m. in pain and got dressed! He ate breakfast around seven and later took his clothes off in the living room, saying his shirt was too tight and his pants too warm. He changed into cooler clothes and took a nap.

On the last day of July, he had another episode. After dinner, I left him sitting in the kitchen while I went outside to water some bushes, gone for just five to seven minutes. When I returned, he was standing at the counter, holding on for dear life, saying he was going to fall. His stool was right behind him, and I tried to convince him to just sit down, but he was afraid! I got his walker, removed the stool, and told him to sit on the walker, showing him where the handles were. He didn't believe me, so I put his hands on the handles. He still wasn't cooperating, and we were getting nowhere, so I called the RN and told her I needed help. She promised to send someone, but it would take that person at least twenty-five minutes to drive across town. So, I retrieved Rick's wheelchair from the garage and canceled the help. With effort, he transferred to the wheelchair, but his feet were dragging on the floor, and we weren't going anywhere.

I raced back to the garage and brought in the footrests. Once they were attached and his feet were off the floor, I wheeled him into the bedroom, where he stayed for the remainder of the night.

A couple of days later, he ate breakfast and then slept for five hours on the couch. Once he was tucked in, I made a trip to the grocery store. When I got back, he was awake and asked how far I had had to go to get to the store. I answered like it was a reasonable question, but deep down inside, it made me realize how much further he had declined. It's impossible to describe how I felt seeing this once-intelligent, well-educated man in this condition. It was beyond sadness.

That same day, he walked from the kitchen to the living room and noticed our two gliders. He commented, "Oh, they have chairs just like ours!"

He went to the bathroom twice that night and wet his clothes and the floor both times! He was adamant that something was wrong with the toilet and insisted he didn't want to leave until HE knew what was wrong with it! I coaxed him into going back to bed both times so I could clean the bathroom again.

The following day, he needed to go to the bathroom and asked me where it was. Then he peeked into his bedroom and wanted to know whose room it was. As he surveyed the bedroom, he commented on the nice bed and asked what size it was. I told him it sure looked comfortable and asked if he wanted to try it out. He thought he would, so he decided to lie down and forgot that he had to go to the bathroom!

He had a bad headache after his nap, so I rubbed some medicated oil on his neck, and he thought it felt better. After lunch, I made him a chocolate sundae. The chocolate got smeared everywhere, so I'm not sure how much he actually ate!

I helped him with a shower one day when the aide wasn't coming, but he didn't like the way I did anything. He complained the whole time, but at least he was clean! He needed help getting dressed, and then I gave him a shave. This was no easy job and not fun for either one of us!

He wore pull-ups to bed that night after I explained that it would help me if I didn't have to scrub the floor in the middle of the night. All went well until 5:30 the next morning!

I woke up as he entered my bedroom with his walker. I got up and asked him what he needed, and he said he was looking for me. We went to the kitchen, where I noticed all the ceiling lights were on. He opened the refrigerator, got the chocolate milk out, poured himself a glass, and took some crackers from the pantry. He put them on the seat of his walker and returned to his room. I turned out the lights and went back to bed.

When I finally got up and went to check on him, I found six to eight pairs of underwear and five to six pairs of pajamas on his bed. I asked him what he was doing, and he said he was packing to go! A while later, while we were eating breakfast, he asked, "What is this place called?" I told him it was our home, and he said, "I couldn't remember where we lived." I started quizzing him, and, surprisingly, he got a lot of the questions correct, but he still thought we lived in "another town" close by, where we had moved from.

Later, while I was watching TV in my room, he came in with his walker and said he needed to use my bathroom. I asked why, and he said his was busy. I told him, "We're the only two people here," but he replied, "But the door is closed!" Then he turned and headed toward his own bathroom!

His behavior was unpredictable and exhausting, some days more than others! He came into my bedroom at 1:18 in the morning. I knew what time it was because I quickly looked at the clock on the nightstand. As usual, all the ceiling lights were on in the rest of the house. I quietly asked him what he needed, and he said he was looking for the stairs. I told him we didn't have any and that he needed to go back to bed. He asked, "Where is it?" So, I got up and took him back to his room.

It happened all over again at 7:00. He came into my room and said it was 9:00. He went into the kitchen, poured himself some juice, and fixed himself a dish of cottage cheese—something he hadn't done in months! When I got up, I found him walking in circles, so I told him to sit while I finished fixing his breakfast. I asked him how he was feeling, and he said, "Pretty good. I am a little dizzy, though." I wasn't sure about the dizziness, as he hadn't mentioned it for a few days.

It was time for Rick to get another massage from our favorite massage therapist to work out all the kinks and sore muscles. He got much-needed relief that helped reduce the tension in his head and neck. Afterward, he had a chiropractic appointment that helped even more with his neck and ribs, and then he had a dermatology appointment to wrap up our day!

On the way to his recent eye appointment, he put his glasses in the storage compartment of his walker seat. He folded the walker, placed it in the car, and smashed the frames so tightly we couldn't even unfold them. Figure that one out! The glasses were only four months old and completely tweaked! A second pair of tinted glasses was due to be delivered any day, so we took the tweaked ones in to be rescued until the new ones were ready. Surprise! The pros were successful in making them wearable again.

September began with another fall when Rick lost his balance getting ready for bed and bruised his right side, just below the shoulder blade. He had difficulty sleeping, so I applied ice to the area the next morning.

Rick started asking, "Who was that little girl who was here?" I wasn't aware there had been anyone here, but Rick had seen her! It upset him that I never saw the people he did. He even brought it up to one of the RNs, and she told him, "You do realize that those people aren't really here, don't you?" He said he understood, but I suspect he knew that was the answer she wanted to hear.

Another Hospice evaluation was due after six months, and it was a mutual decision to discontinue that level of care at the end of September since he had basically stayed the same without declining any further. He was transferred back to Palliative Care at the beginning of October.

I returned from grocery shopping and noticed the lamp shade by his chair was crooked, some leaves from a plant were on the floor, and the doily under the lamp was upside down. When I asked Rick about it, he told me he had knocked the lamp over! From experience, I knew this only happened when he came out of a deep sleep with his arms flying in all directions. He had startled me out of my wits a couple of times while I was sitting next to him reading or watching TV.

He fell getting out of bed one night but didn't mention it until I noticed his skinned knee the next day. That was his explanation for the knee this time!

There seemed to be a lot of miscommunication with Palliative Care this time around. We had people arriving unannounced or not showing up when expected. Then, we were informed of new changes that Medicare had added. In order to simplify our life and reduce all the traffic in and out of the house, I discontinued Palliative Care in mid-October to see how long we could manage without help. Losing the aide who came to help with showers was our biggest loss.

Rick advised me one day he'd had chest pains after getting out of bed that morning and that it had been hard to breathe. He said the pain wrapped around his chest and lasted about an hour. When I questioned him, he couldn't remember all the details. He said he had gone to the bathroom and sat at his computer until the pain stopped. What confused me was that he hadn't mentioned it at breakfast and waited until 4:30 in the afternoon to tell me.

Other than another trip to InstaCare for plugged ears and a good cleaning, New Year's Eve ended as usual: watching all the fireworks on TV!

CHAPTER 08 | Lost Soul

I started 2021 with my usual optimism, as things seemed to be coasting along smoothly with routine lab work, phlebotomy appointments, dermatology, eye, and foot appointments for his toenails.

In February, he tried to adjust his glasses and popped a lens out. By the time he finished trying to put the lens back in, it took two people at LensCrafters to fix them. By then, the employees and he were on a first-name basis! He also tore a loop off his new leather watch band. Why or how? Don't ask—but he kept working at it until it was a mission accomplished!

His hallucinations worsened that February. He asked me about all the kids he thought I watched at night, and he saw kitty cats, dogs, and sometimes older people in the house every day. One evening, he saw many people in the living room from where he was sitting in the kitchen. He was very afraid of all these people he was seeing. My daughter Beth was visiting at the time, and she took him by the hand to show him there was no one else in the house except the three of us. She took him through every room and turned on the lights so he could see there was nothing to be afraid of. He finally calmed down, but it was one of his most frightening experiences. Earlier that day, he had also seen older kids outside peeking in the kitchen window.

He fell on the hardwood floor in the hallway at about 11:30 one night, trying to get to the kitchen without his walker. He skinned the same knee that had a scab on it from a fall weeks earlier, and his left arm was sore for days after this fall.

We visited our primary physician and told him how bad the hallucinations had become, and he spoke "cold turkey" to both of us. Based on his experience, the progression from severe hallucinations with advanced dementia to the stage of needing total care was about nine months.

He said it would go downhill quickly from this point and told me to watch for signs of wandering and incontinence, both of which were already in full swing. He recommended Home Care again, so I would have "someone" to call in an emergency. He also informed me that I wouldn't be able to care for him by myself once he needed full care.

That news put me in high-alert mode. I felt I needed to have a plan, but I wasn't sure where to start.

He already had a Veterans Administration ID card, and we had visited the VA Home several years earlier. They gave us a package with an application and information but left us with the understanding that he didn't qualify to live there based on the dates he was in the Air Force. However, a representative from the VA Office in Salt Lake City, where he received his ID card, disagreed. Since I didn't feel he was close to needing to be moved to any facility at that time, the application was filed away and never submitted.

It was time to dig that application out of the file and fill it out because the clock was now ticking. Once filled out, we delivered it to the VA Home and were told it would be a three-year wait for Rick because his disability was not military-related. They took the application, but I knew in my heart that Rick wouldn't be here in three years.

I met with one memory-care administrator, took a tour of the facility, and received information on pricing. When I left, I knew Rick would never live there—not because of the money, but because it felt cold and uninviting. I still didn't have a plan, but I didn't close the door on suggestions. In my heart, I turned it over to God and trusted Him to guide me in the right direction, at the right time, and in what would be best for Rick.

Donna and Dave came for a couple of days shortly after our discussion with the doctor. Since they had been involved with his care after the first stroke in California, they were cognizant of his condition.

On March 1st, he ordered a little girl to leave the house and threw a pillow at her! At lunch, he was proud of himself for telling her to leave and didn't understand why "they" thought they could just come into the house anytime they liked. That evening, when I got up to go to bed, he saw a young couple sitting with me on the loveseat and asked if I was going to let them stay all night. When I told him no one else was here, he said I was being difficult!

The next morning at breakfast, he asked me about the young girls who had been here. I said, "I don't know because I didn't see them, and they didn't talk to me." He said they had looked at him and had washed their hair. I asked, "How do you know?" and he said, "Because they had wet hair with towels wrapped around their heads." I finally told him not to get upset with them or me because they weren't here to hurt us. It annoyed him the most that none of these visitors ever asked permission to come into our house.

Not long after, he woke up during the night and saw dirt and mud everywhere on the floor in his bedroom, hallway, and bathroom. He believed his pajamas were covered in mud, so he put clean ones on. He told me about it the next morning, and I was thankful he hadn't come into my room and asked me to scrub the floors!

We had to make another trip back to LensCrafters to put a lens back in his dark glasses and a new screw as well. He said it had also happened the week before, though he said he had popped that one back in himself. I wasn't sure anymore if the things he told me were the result of his imagination or a spark of clear memory.

After buying a new leather band for his talking watch (yes, the one he managed to pull a loop off), it stopped talking and was off by a few minutes. When daylight savings time rolled around, it didn't switch to the new time. So, we went shopping for a new watch. This adventure was actually fun, as he knew exactly what he was looking for and where he wanted to buy it. To my amazement, he found the perfect watch at the very store he knew would have it!

I ordered a new bookcase that was delivered to the front porch while I was gone. Rick was home, and I still hoped he'd stay out of trouble during the short absences I had to make! At that point in his journey, I felt he could be left alone for a brief time—and I mean brief!

Superman Rick carried that heavy box into the house by himself and was all enthused about breaking the box open to assemble the bookcase when I got home. Since we were expecting a visit from his middle daughter and her family in the next few days, that was a task I thought we would ask our grandson to help with.

The day after he carried that heavy box inside, his right elbow was in lots of pain. After a pain pill and the heating pad, he slept and felt better the next day. Then he kept scratching his upper arm until it was bloody. I never knew why, and he had no explanation. To top it off, there were seven more bloody spots he had scratched raw the day after that! That big problem eventually cleared up with over-the-counter ointment.

In hindsight, I believe my grieving started when the doctor said Rick would go downhill rapidly in the next nine months. Rick didn't talk about it much, and I tried to live each day, trying not to dwell on it. His four children took the news as seriously as I did, and all wanted to visit as soon as they could. I understood the urgency they felt in wanting to see a dad they loved and admired to the core. I had also been a daughter to a dad I felt the same way about.

Rick tired easily and took naps often. It became a daily occurrence for him to disappear, and I would find him asleep on his bed or in his chair while watching TV. If friends came to see him, they kept their visits short, but his children lived too far away for just brief visits. Although they stayed in hotels and often found local activities to occupy some of their time, long visits wore him out because he felt the need to stay awake while they were here. As much as he fought to keep his eyes open, he was caught a few times nodding off in his chair anyway!

Rick's middle daughter Nan, husband Jim, and their three children were not able to visit during these final months, but when they had come a few times before, they accomplished many house repairs that were greatly appreciated. Nan also took on the task during one of their visits to install a kitchen backsplash that became a beautiful upgrade. They were always doing something to help us when they came!

Beth only had a two-hour drive, so she often came up for the day. She became my "rock" during these difficult months. She always brought big bouquets for each of us, brought meals and food items, bought us both an Alexa and set it up, and helped me in numerous other ways. She listened while I talked and vented my fears and frustrations. Between her visits, she called regularly and was always available when I called her. I unloaded a lot onto her, and in hindsight, I know I overloaded her.

Jess and his family arrived for a couple of days in April. Their new baby and little toddler—

our two youngest grandchildren—kept us entertained!

Rick started moving furniture in his bedroom again and needed a chiropractic adjustment afterward. He still thought he could lift things and push stuff around without consequences, and by the end of the day, he was overly tired. While he was sitting in his chair that evening in the living room, he saw a kitten by his foot and actually began petting it!

The next day, he saw lots of people in the house and remarked that he saw the boy who had been peeking in the kitchen window several weeks before. He said he hadn't seen the boy in a while. He also saw the back of an older man with a white crew cut and said that man hadn't been here before. I asked him if he saw any familiar faces, like his mom. He said, "No, but it would be nice to see her!"

While he spent the next day moving things in his room again, he had all the cords underneath his armoire tangled up and didn't know where they had been or where they needed to go.

I fell asleep on the loveseat that evening, and he woke me up, asking when we were going home. I told him we were home and to go to bed, but he said he would when we got home! Shortly thereafter, he realized we were home but said all the furniture was different. He came to his senses and even apologized.

Donna, Dave, their two daughters, and a son-in-law visited us for a couple of days, and we did some sightseeing with them. Rick overextended himself trying to keep up with his walker and later paid the price with extreme pain in his legs and feet. He always tried to look strong for others, even when he was in pain.

The following week, I was finally able to get some sleep on the couch. My energy level had dropped, and I was dragging my heels more each day. At 4:50 in the morning, I saw the kitchen lights on. When I asked Rick why he was up so early, he was completely disoriented. He said, "The altitude is bothering my head, and my eyes don't want to focus. This elevation is making me dizzy! How are we going to get off this mountain?" I reached him and explained where we were, but his confusion continued. He told me he had gone through a long tunnel on a tour with other people. When they reached the end of the tunnel, they came out on the top of this mountain. He kept asking me how we were going to get down! His blood pressure was slightly elevated, but his sugar was normal.

The next night, he dreamed that he was off the mountain, walking on flat land with two other people. He saw our house with no roof and went inside. Once he was in his bedroom, he realized where he was and went to the bathroom. Things were familiar, but it seemed strange that he was dreaming about the mountain again.

He had a phlebotomy appointment and explained those dreams to the RN who was drawing his 500 ml of blood. She was amazed at how vividly he remembered those dreams, noting that most dementia patients wouldn't recall them so clearly.

***

On May 4th, I adopted a nine-week-old Aussiepoo and named her Gidget. This was not a planned adoption, nor had I ever intended to get another dog! I randomly walked into the puppy store and spotted her trying to get my attention. As she danced up and down and all around the plexiglass enclosure, I could almost hear her saying, "Pick me, pick me!" I asked which one was the female, as her brother was with her. When they told me that the little furry puppy who wanted my attention was the female, I agreed to hold her. From the moment I held her, she wouldn't stop giving me kisses. To prove she was all girl, she even loved my earrings! When they asked if I wanted to take her home, I gave it a long thought and then blurted out, "I'll take her!"

When I walked into the house holding this adorable three-pound puppy, all adorned with a big pink ribbon around her neck, the look on Rick's face was priceless! A big bonus was that she already knew how to use a potty pad! We introduced her to our backyard and took lots of pictures to document the occasion, and Rick said it was the happiest day of his life!

About a week later, I woke up feeling quite sick with no appetite, a headache, body aches, a slight fever, nausea, a very dry mouth, and extreme thirst. I went to see a doctor three days later and was told it was a virus that couldn't be treated unless I had had the fever for at least a week. The doctor was also hesitant to prescribe more antibiotics since I had just finished a course after some dental work. When I asked how he could tell the difference between a bacterial infection and a virus, his answer was that it came from years of experience. I left the office and went home feeling as bad as I had when I arrived.

As I continued to feel worse, Beth offered to come up that weekend and take Gidget home for a couple of weeks until I felt better. I didn't hesitate to accept her offer. By the time the weekend came, I was extremely sick and barely cared about what was happening around me. Rick managed to make himself peanut butter and jelly sandwiches, cold cereal, or anything else quick and easy.

When Beth arrived, she recognized how serious my condition was and said she wouldn't leave until she took me to the ER. I knew if I didn't go, I wouldn't be around much longer. I felt as if I were fading away—so peaceful, so relaxed. I had to get help, so I managed to throw some clothes on and let her drive me to the hospital.

As I lay there having blood drawn and other tests, Beth told the doctor she had never seen me like that before. Believe me, I had never felt like that before, either. The diagnosis came back as E. coli bacteria, which had already entered my bloodstream! They wanted to admit me, but I refused because I needed to take care of Rick at home. They ran a blood culture to confirm the diagnosis over the next couple of days, but they started me on a prescription right away that would attack the bacteria, if they were correct. Fortunately, I responded to the medication, and the culture later confirmed it was E. coli. The hospital called three times during that week to check on me, and it took several weeks for me to fully recover.

Beth had taken Gidget home temporarily, but while recovering from E. coli, I realized I wasn't in a position to take care of both of us and Gidget at the time. A new puppy demanded more time and energy than I had to give. So, Gidget continued living with Beth, and we agreed to co-parent, meaning I would still help with any future vet bills.

Rick missed his little Gidget and kept asking when she was coming home. I eventually had to be honest with him, explaining that I had too much on my plate to care for her right then, but she would visit often. He looked forward to those visits and fully enjoyed the time they spent together.

***

A milestone was approaching, and Rick would soon be celebrating his eightieth birthday—the big 8-0! I gave this one a lot of thought, trying to decide what we could do to make it extra special. After all, what do you get someone who doesn't need anything? He had made it clear to me years ago that he couldn't see well enough to read the cards given to him, no longer enjoyed big-boy toys or gadgets, and never thought it was appropriate to give or receive clothes as a gift! I had been raised differently, so it wasn't always easy to choose something for him. Still, he always showed his appreciation and extended heartfelt thank-yous to everyone who celebrated with him!

I decided we were going to indulge in food all week, and we'd go out to lunch every day during his birthday week! I gave him a "blank check" to pick his favorite restaurants, and that put a huge smile on his face right away. Bells and whistles started going off in his head as he eagerly blurted out one place after another. The little boy in him was already planning a big week of celebration!

Of course, he still needed something to open on his big day! See's sugar-free walnut clusters made his mouth water, but he was generous and offered me one piece before stashing the rest in his room. Dairy Queen was a favorite for both of us, so an ice-cream cake was waiting in our freezer, ready for us to enjoy a slice each day after lunch.

One of his first choices was the Sizzler in Cedar City. It was always a pleasant drive, and our favorite meal was their Malibu Chicken. He also picked Ernesto's Mexican restaurant, where we'd been regulars for over twenty years. Another day, it was Panda Garden for Chinese food. Magleby's, a fine-dining spot in a local hotel, was his pick for its peaceful ambiance. His list wouldn't have been complete without the Pasta Factory, with its pasta lunch specials. The Golden Corral was another favorite, and Rick couldn't resist piling his plate high. If chocolate pie was available at the dessert bar, he'd go for it—after all, his Mama had raised him on homemade chocolate pie.

The celebration didn't stop with food. Rick received calls, cards, and texts. Beth sent him a case of snacks from Amazon, packed with a variety of chips! His youngest daughter and her family came to visit, bringing him two freshly-baked Marie Callender pies—chocolate and banana cream. They also brought mixed nuts, chocolate cookies, and treated him to lunch at Culver's! Since his birthday was so close to Father's Day, June was always a double celebration for him. Beth came for a visit as well, and we wrapped up the birthday week at Texas Roadhouse. To my knowledge, this was one of Rick's happiest and most memorable birthdays. I know because he told so many people about it for months afterward!

In the meantime, my strength and energy hadn't been returning like I'd hoped. I was overdue for my cardiology appointment because of a computer issue in their office. When I finally saw the doctor in July, I explained the symptoms I'd been experiencing along with some other health issues that had developed in recent months. After undergoing heart tests later that month, I received a call from the doctor's office the next day—they wanted me at the hospital first thing Monday morning for an angiogram. I was told to bring an overnight bag in case I needed to be admitted afterward.

Preparing for the unknown, Beth came to be with me at the hospital while Donna flew in to take care of her dad. I ended up receiving five stents that day, bringing my total to six.

Needless to say, I was admitted overnight and went home the next day. After Beth and Donna left, I resumed my normal duties as usual.

I did six follow-up cardio rehab visits at the hospital but, unfortunately, wasn't consistent in keeping up with cardio exercises afterward. Walking on my treadmill at home was highly encouraged, but I found other things always seemed to take priority. As a result, I didn't build up my heart muscle or increase my stamina, and daily chores continued to wear me out. I was reminded that caregivers can be the first to to go due to stress, self-neglect, and lack of sleep.

Rick was a true American and had never missed a chance to vote for his favorite candidates. When his ballot arrived for an upcoming election, I found him practicing his signature over and over to sign his name. He was not able to write his name at all and became so frustrated that he threw the ballot aside and never voted again.

He finally got an appointment with a new VA doctor in St. George. While we kept our primary physician, the VA was able to provide prescriptions that our regular insurance didn't cover, which was a huge relief and a big step forward in getting the support we needed.

Rick always asked me lots of questions, often coming out of nowhere! Food must have been on his mind when he asked, "Do we still have an Applebee's?" That was followed by the dessert question, "Do we still have that place that makes ice cream?" I'm sure he meant the Blue Bunny factory, which had been gone from our area for years.

When I handed Rick a laundry bag full of my white dirty clothes that included two dirty hand towels, I asked him to add his whites to the bag. He misunderstood and came back asking, "Do you want me to fold your clothes too?" He had folded the two hand towels and put them in his linen closet, leaving his dirty clothes out of the bag entirely.

The vision in his good eye had started worsening with more blurriness since his last Avastin injection, so the retina doctor switched him to the more expensive Eyelea injections. By the following visit, the swelling had gone down some, so the plan was to continue with Eyelea and see if he could go longer between injections. With the help of the doctor's office, we applied for and received a grant to help cover the cost of the treatments. After a few Eyelea injections, the less-expensive Avastin injections continued since there was no significant change in his vision.

On September 24th, at around 4:30 a.m., Rick got up to go to the bathroom and thought he heard a child in the living room. Since we were dog-sitting Gidget at the time, she barked when she heard him. Naturally, I got up too and met Rick just as he turned on the kitchen light. When I asked what he was doing up at that hour, he said he was lost. I told him he needed to go back to bed, but he wasn't sure where his bedroom was. He was so confused that I had to help him find it. By the time he got up at seven, everything was back to normal.

About a week later, he complained of sore shoulders and arms when he went to bed. When I asked how long he'd felt like that, he said it had been about a week! He asked for a pain pill, but he had already taken acetaminophen and a sleep aid, so I wouldn't give him anything else. I offered the heating pad instead, but he declined, saying, "No, it won't help." Another trip to the chiropractor ended up being just what he needed!

***

It was October 9th when Rick showed me that he had wires coming out of his right arm. He had been picking at two areas that had started to bleed, so I put band-aids on them. His arm hurt above the right elbow, and he believed those wires were coming from the surgery site where his new shoulder was located. I tried to reassure him that there were no wires, but it quickly turned into a debate.

"Yes, I do!" he insisted.

"No, you don't," I replied.

He pulled the vacuum out of the hall closet one other day and was busy vacuuming his bedroom carpet when I walked in. I was surprised to see him working so hard and couldn't understand what had prompted this until he explained there were piles of sand everywhere!

Then came the issue with his bed slats. He told me that the middle slat under his bed had fallen out of the frame and was now on the floor, making the bed uneven. I got down on my hands and knees to inspect the problem, only to discover that the bed didn't even have slats!

And there was more! He told me, "The cat just threw up all over the floor!"—even though we didn't have a cat. I told him I'd clean up the mess, and that seemed to satisfy him for the time being.

That same evening, on October 17th, he whispered in my ear that there were three guys sitting on the floor watching TV. Then they disappeared, but Rick was convinced they had not come through the front door and didn't think they had gone out that door either.

After a routine dental appointment for X-rays and a cleaning, it was discovered that Rick had a broken filling that would need to be replaced at a later date.

On October 22nd, at 5:40 in the morning, he turned on the living room and kitchen lights again. As usual, I got up and asked him what he was doing. He smiled pleasantly and kept looking around the house, saying, "This is a nice place!" I asked if he was lost, but he just said he was looking for me. He then looked into the living room and commented on how nice it was, adding, "It looks a lot like ours, same finish!" I checked his blood sugar, and it was a little low, so I made him some breakfast. As he ate, I asked him when he had gotten up, and he replied, "When you came in and got me!"

I noticed he hadn't been wearing his glasses lately. When I asked him about it, he admitted he couldn't find them despite searching everywhere. I went into his room and started looking through his dresser and all the glass cases. He snapped at me, "I've already looked there!" I found one pair and tried to convince him they were one of his two new ones.

"NO, THEY AREN'T," he yelled.

I found another pair, and again, the same response. He didn't remember what his glasses looked like or how dark the tint was on the new ones. Frustrated, I left the room. A little while later, he came out wearing one of the pairs I had found. He seemed to have forgotten the feud and acted as though everything was status quo!

I was worn out and said I was going to bed, and he asked if I was going to let the girls stay with their boyfriends! Too tired to deal with that again, I just kept walking, which irritated him.

October had been an active month, and the twenty-fourth was no different. That afternoon, he came into the living room carrying his trash can, trying to scoop up a bug. When I called him for lunch, he ignored me, and I told him to forget about the bugs! In his mind, he already had two big ones in the trash can. Still, he decided lunch wasn't a bad idea and brought the can with him, proudly showing me one bug sitting right on top. While eating, he kept scanning the floor and even got off his stool at one point to pick up another one!

He spent a few hours in his room listening to a new audio tape. As dusk fell, he came into the living room, snacked on some Trail Mix that I had put beside his chair, and casually mentioned the two girls who had been here earlier. He thought I had seen them too. I responded, "I didn't see them and didn't talk to them." He said they didn't talk to him, and he didn't talk to them either, but he was convinced I knew about their visit because he saw me interacting with them! Curious, I asked what they looked like, and he described them in detail. One was older, nicely dressed, and the younger girl wore a hat and coat. He truly believed that I had been involved with those girls and all the other kids who showed up in the house.

I called him for lunch on another day and found him searching around his chair in the living room, looking underneath and behind it, along with the footstool and table. Once again, he was seeing bugs everywhere. I told him to come into the kitchen and eat, which he did. But he kept looking at all the bugs on the kitchen floor as well. At one point, he even stood up to take a closer look and told me we needed to get the "bug guy" out here to take care of them.

Disgusted with himself, he admitted he didn't know what was going on and needed to make himself know that those things he was seeing weren't really there. I reminded him of what the doctor had said back in February: that the journey he was on wouldn't get better, and if we saw the doctor again, he would say the same thing.

That day, Rick also saw a mouse trap with a small critter pleading for help. He asked if I had put the trap there, as he got up to show me where it was. It took a lot of convincing for him to get his mind on something else, but that's what I had to do. Just changing the subject and diverting his attention elsewhere sometimes worked!

I could never predict what would come out of his mouth next. While I was at the kitchen sink cleaning up the dinner dishes, Rick quietly whispered, "Did you see that young man just now?" He said the guy was in pajamas and must have been looking for food. "Nice looking," Rick remarked, as he sat in his own pajamas, which he often wore before dark.

When I finally took a break and had the kitchen cleaned up, I went in to watch a little TV. I thought, *"Oh, how relaxing a back rub would feel about now!"* Rick used to be more than willing to give me a back rub, but those days had slowly disappeared. The rubs became shorter, with longer intervals in between. He didn't offer as many, and I didn't ask as often. It got to the point where if he did agree to rub my back, I knew he would stop within a few minutes and slump over sound asleep!

The World Series started that same evening between the Atlanta Braves and the Houston Astros, but Rick was seriously confused and said he would be rooting for the Dodgers!

He struggled using the remote while trying to change channels and, at one point, spotted something on the floor with two wings. I told him to step on it, but he said it was too big.

Rick had been dealing with loose stools for about a week, so I cut out his Vitamin C, added Pepto Bismol when he asked, and later switched to Imodium. The issue persisted on and off, day and night.

As we ate lunch one day, he said, "If we ever move back to Vegas, maybe we can go to one of those churches we like!" We had never lived in Vegas, but we had visited two churches there. At least he was thinking positively and trying to plan ahead.

Beth was preparing to move into her new house, awaiting the completion of renovations. I had updated Rick on her progress, but I soon realized he misunderstood. He asked when *our* place would be ready for us to move into!

Towards the end of October, Rick found his old eye patch and started wearing it. He believed he had solved the "monster" problem, because he hadn't seen any since putting it on. Later, though, he sadly asked if he had it on correctly, because he had just seen three bugs in his room! He thought the problem was the patch, so now he wanted a new one. To satisfy him, I went online, found several options, and ordered one he liked.

I hired a lady to come in once a month to clean the floors. One day, while she worked, we sat outside on the patio. Rick became irritated when he thought he heard kids inside and wondered if they had come with her. When she stepped outside to say she had finished, Rick pointed towards the house and asked if those kids were hers. She was shocked and told him, "No, they're not mine," unaware of how much Rick's condition had declined. After walking her to the door, I updated her on his condition, letting her know that he was now hearing and seeing imaginary kids in the house.

The doctor prescribed a new pill for schizophrenia. Earlier in the evening, Rick had trouble walking and speaking clearly. After he went to bed, I heard him muttering to himself, but when I checked, he was sound asleep. I turned on the light and held his hand, but he didn't respond. He eventually woke up as I took his blood pressure, which was normal, and I helped him to the bathroom and back to bed.

About an hour later, I heard him heading to the bathroom again. It sounded like his usual routine of shutting the door and flushing the toilet, so I stayed put and listened. When he didn't come out, I waited a little while before knocking and asking if he needed help. He said, "Yes!" He hadn't made it to the bathroom in time and was sitting on the stool with his pajamas and underwear on the floor! After assisting him to clean up, I helped him back to bed and then returned to clean up the bathroom.

***

The following morning, he was ready to eat breakfast when he got up. He wanted to take a shower and preferred to do it by himself! I supervised as little as possible so he wouldn't think I was interfering. Afterwards, he was wiped out but clean, as far as I knew.

Debbie and Beth came for a visit that day and brought Gidget. Rick was out on the patio when they arrived and was so excited to see Gidget that he lost his balance with the walker and fell to his knees on the cement. Debbie caught him before he hurt himself further, but he still ended up with two skinned knees.

We all sat down to eat, but Rick was distracted when he saw a number of people outside. His eating habits were especially compromised that day, and he didn't seem to remember any of the good table manners he once had. However, we all rode the waves with him as he continued his long journey.

On the last day of October, he woke up and said he had slept well and had not gotten up once during the night! As he sat at the counter, ready to eat breakfast, he accidentally tipped over his oatmeal, which went all down his pajamas, the stool, and the floor. I helped him change his pajamas, fixed him a bowl of cold cereal, and had him sit at the table. It upset him that he couldn't sit on his stool at the counter while I cleaned the oatmeal off the floor.

After he finished breakfast, I thought he went into his bedroom. About an hour later, I went in to check on him and found him in the bathroom. Apparently, he had been in there since he had left the kitchen, so I asked if he needed help. Yes, he did! I gave him a wet rag to clean himself up and then helped him to his room.

He explained that he saw bugs on the bathroom floor, so he didn't want to put his feet down. He wanted to get on his bed because there were also bugs all over his bedroom floor! He seemed satisfied after I turned the TV on and closed the blinds before I left the room.

He went out back and said how gorgeous everything looked and was quite surprised to learn it was his yard! He remarked that he thought it looked familiar and continued to compliment me on what a good job I had done making the house so beautiful. He said he really loved it!

It was October, and nothing was different at our house. The World Series was on TV, and Rick was very busy doing something with his hands while looking down at the floor. I asked him what he was doing but couldn't quite understand his explanation. It looked like he was trying to reel in a fish on his pole, but he said, "No." Or was he pulling taffy? No, that wasn't it, either. Oh well, it kept him busy, and looked like he was having fun!

He made another trip to the bathroom, and he saw a line on the floor. I never knew exactly what kind of line it was and couldn't understand what he was trying to tell me. Those bugs were still on the bathroom floor, so he kept swatting at them with his shoe. When I tried to help him, he got upset with me because "he needed to cut that wire that was coming through the wall!" His speech was very slurred.

I heard him hitting the floor with his shoe at 12:30 in the morning on November 1st. By then, I usually slept on the couch every night so I could hear everything coming from his side of the house. I made a mad dash to his room! He was seeing bugs everywhere and had to go to the bathroom. I said there were no bugs and reminded him that the RN had said they're really not there, but he said he didn't care what she had said! So, I helped him into the bathroom, but he didn't need my help in there this time. He was hesitant about going back into his room and said he didn't think he would be able to sleep in there. I coaxed him onto the bed, turned his TV on to Escape music, and turned the light off. After I left the room, he was still talking – maybe telling the bugs to leave!

At 2:30, he got up and quietly made his way to the front door with only socks on his feet and no walker, opened it, and closed it! I have no idea why I didn't wake up before he got to the door, because I was sleeping on the couch to make sure I didn't miss anything! No doubt, it was probably exhaustion on my part. At any rate, Rick said he didn't know where he wanted to go, so I escorted him back to bed. I couldn't understand what he was trying to say, and he got upset with me when I was trying to help. Having him open the front door was a new adventure for him, and it was a real eye-opener for me to realize what could have happened if I hadn't been right there. All the "what ifs" went through my mind, and I realized then that I could no longer leave him alone!

At 4:45, I heard him awake in his room. The lights didn't go on this time, so I tried to doze off again. Then he came into the living room, again with only socks on his feet and no walker, then fell. He said something about sleepwalking, as far as I could understand, so I asked him if he was awake. As he sat on the floor, he responded in a loud voice, 'I AM NOW!" He sat there for a while and finally scooted over to the couch and got himself up while I turned on the TV. Helping him up was something I wasn't able to do!

At breakfast, he was not only seeing bugs, but birds too. The world he was in at this point must have been very lonely and scary for him. He was in a place all by himself where no one could understand how he felt or see all the things he was seeing. It had to be frustrating when no one seemed to believe him, and it felt the same for me, knowing that I couldn't reach him anymore!

While I was getting ready for a follow-up cardio appointment, Rick was in the living room talking to another kitty! Up until that day, I felt pretty confident that he would be okay by himself for short periods of time, and I always told myself I would know when he couldn't be left alone anymore. After last night, today was that day!

We arrived for my appointment, and Rick used his walker to go in with me. While we were in the exam room waiting for the PA to arrive, he was fiercely scratching both of his hands and wouldn't stop. I asked, "What in the world are you doing?" As he kept scratching, he said, "I'm trying to get all this dirt off my hands." He pointed at the handles of his walker and tried to show me all the dirt they had on them. I told him he needed to stop or he would scratch them raw, but no one could have convinced him otherwise.

The PA came into the room with one of her assistants. They took my vitals and were alarmed that my blood pressure was up. They took it again and became quite concerned. All of a sudden, one of them said, "Oh, his hand is bleeding!" She grabbed a paper towel and handed it to him while I retrieved a band-aid from my purse.

Of course, my blood pressure was up. They had no idea what my life was like at that point! So, they did their job and increased my medications.

We turned out the lights about ten o'clock that night and went our separate ways for the night. Not long after, I heard him yelling for me. It was the first time I had heard a frantic call for help like that. I raced into his bedroom and found him half-sitting on the edge of the bed, very out of breath after falling and getting himself up partway. He tried to lie back down and did, in a sort of way, but he had no energy and couldn't scoot himself up far enough to be completely on the bed. After I helped scoot him up a little more, he was breathing hard and stared up at the ceiling with a look in his eyes that I had never seen before. As I watched, it appeared that he was seeing "something!"

He said he had to go to the bathroom, so I tried to help him sit up to get his walker. He couldn't do it, and he couldn't stand on his legs either.

I called the RN from Home Care, and she suggested I help him with a urinal. Rick didn't want to use it because he saw a lot of people in the room! He got frustrated and wanted to use the bathroom! He kept trying to tug at his walker and ended up on the floor again. I tried to help him get back up, but there was no use. He didn't have an ounce of energy left in him! That's when I called 9-1-1.

Paramedics arrived within minutes and got Rick up on the bed. They took his vitals, and all the numbers seemed normal until they realized there was a big fluctuation in his blood pressure between sitting up and lying down. No one could understand what he was trying to say, and he was unable to stand on his legs. So, he was loaded up and transported to the hospital at eleven o'clock that night.

By the time I arrived at the hospital, they had examined him and done lab work. He was very weak, asleep, maybe unconscious, but appeared to be quite comfortable. I sat beside the bed, watching him and waiting for an update on his condition. He never woke to converse with me, and I sat there hour after hour.

Finally, a social worker came in at about 3 a.m. and introduced herself. I knew his condition had deteriorated and was serious, but it was still shocking to hear the news she was about to deliver.

They felt it was time to put Rick on Hospice again, and I just sat there listening in a fog. It didn't occur to me to ask any questions; I didn't have any! She further explained that they would gradually wean him off all his medications with Hospice care and asked if I understood what she was saying. I slowly nodded, "Yes." In my heart, I knew this was the end!

I tried to stay calm and strong after hearing that Rick was actually at the end of his journey. We had been told that he would decline quickly within the next nine months after his hallucinations had become so bad, and here we were nine months later. I had been warned that Rick would get worse, and

I would not be able to care for him by myself when that time came. The thoughts went through my mind, *"How bad is 'worse'?" "When will 'worse' arrive?" "How should I prepare?" "How am I supposed to know what I don't know?"*

I kept turning to my Holy Savior for guidance, support, and strength. Even when I felt completely alone, I knew God was there and in charge. I never lost touch with Him and prayed He would continue to work through Rick's medical staff in these final days.

As I tried to stay strong on the outside, sometimes I felt like I was falling apart on the inside. There were times when I had serious talks with God and moments when my emotions exploded. He and I were in this together, and I knew He was there holding me up when I didn't think I could go any further. Like I had been warned months earlier, sometimes the Caregivers are the first to go. I was determined to stay strong, not only for Rick but determined that this was not going to take me too!

Rick was admitted to the Neurology Unit at 4:30 that morning. Once transferred upstairs, I went home but received a call from a PA several hours later asking for an update on Rick's activities over the last few days and a list of current medications. They did a CAT scan, and it was considered normal. It also showed a slightly enlarged heart, but it was not of concern at that point.

When I arrived for a visit, Rick was sitting in his chair on a bed alarm after he had gotten out of bed and tried walking to the door earlier. When he was transported to the ER, he was unable to stand on his legs; now he could! His speech was a little better but still quite slurred, and I was not able to understand a lot of what he said. The bugs were still bothering him at the hospital, and he saw them in his food, which sat untouched on the table beside him. The floor was covered with them as well, and Rick was obviously very confused.

When I was ready to leave, he said he was ready to go anytime I was. He became agitated when I explained that I couldn't take him with me, so I stayed while they put him back in bed. But he resisted and said he didn't plan to stay there. It was no use trying to explain that I needed to go home and get some sleep but would come back to see him. There was no reasoning with him! He swung at me just before I left and was very upset with life!

The RN called me at 9:10 that night and put Rick on the phone. I started my conversation with Rick by asking, "Who is this?" He replied in a somewhat-improved slurred voice, "Why, this is your son!" He said he didn't want to sleep there because there were people "going at it" down the hall, and he wanted to leave. I gave him a pep talk, and then he didn't want to talk to me anymore. He said he would try to make the best of it and handed the phone back to the RN!

When I arrived about noon the next day, the IV was out, the heart monitor was gone, and he was asleep. His speech was better, and they said he felt pretty good after having a shower that morning, with no hallucinations so far!

The Neurologist came in and discussed Rick's transition to Hospice. They offered me five days of Respite Care and explained it would be paid by Medicare. They would keep Rick in the same room and adjust his medications during that time. I was so grateful to receive that benefit, and it gave me an opportunity to relax and get some much-needed rest. Having those five days without worrying from day to day felt like a gift!

***

The following day, I met with the Hospice team. Rick would receive comfort care, and they explained what was included in the package that would be delivered to the house when he was discharged. An RN would be assigned, an aide would come to bathe him, a chaplain would offer prayer and comfort, and a social worker would help with medical supplies, among other things.

Rick seemed fine at noon when I visited him, but all the bugs returned later that day. I received a report that Rick had gotten "short" with an aide, so they gave him a sleeping pill. After he woke, the bugs were gone!

The doctor called early the next morning and said Rick had had a very bad night with hitting and kicking. The doctor had contacted a psychiatrist for advice on medication to control this behavior, and they made an adjustment. He further explained that they were glad this happened while Rick was still in the hospital, so they could get it under control before sending him home. I expressed my fear of this behavior when he came home because this was a new side of Rick I had only recently witnessed and experienced. The young Rick had never been violent.

There was a possibility that Rick would be transferred to a rehab facility if the behavior continued. In the meantime, the doctor said they had someone keeping an eye on him while he sat in his chair with slight restraints. When I arrived at noon, Josh had been sitting with Rick since seven that morning.

Josh said Rick had torn off his gown and didn't want a blanket. When I walked into the room, Rick was lying on his bed, wearing only a diaper. He refused breakfast and insisted he was going to get out of bed, but he was in no condition to be up. I talked to him, and so did others, but there was no reasoning with him.

At this point, he was being watched by a Patient Monitoring Camera (PMC) in his room. The social worker called and said she understood that I wanted Rick transferred to a nursing facility upon discharge. I clarified that I hadn't said that; the doctor had mentioned it might be necessary. She recommended I start looking into different facilities, which felt like an overwhelming burden. Some facilities were unavailable due to Covid restrictions, one of which required a fourteen-day quarantine for those who had not received "the" shots. In the end, there was really no option but to bring him home.

He insisted on walking to the bathroom, and it took three people to assist him. Afterwards, they put him in his chair. He ate some lunch, drank some apple juice and a little soda, and was able to swallow a blood pressure pill. When I returned after a short absence, he was asleep in the chair. The young aide who was sitting with him had put a blanket around him, and he was still asleep in his chair when I left at 8 p.m.

I arrived a 10:30 the next morning, and the doctor said Rick had had another "testy" night. They had increased his new medication. He had eaten breakfast, taken a shower, was in a fresh gown, and sleeping in a clean bed when I entered his room.

He was awake and alert when his youngest daughter arrived for a visit. At her request, a nurse brought his walker so they could take a walk down the hall. He had never shown a desire to do that before and, up to that point, had not been in any condition to be taking a stroll, but she said he had asked! Whatever transpired, I didn't hear it, and he returned safely without any mishaps.

After being awake for a long time that afternoon, Rick started seeing bugs and spiders crawling all over the floor and in his bed at sundown. Seeing spiders was a new addition. He was so terrified that he ordered the nurse to move the furniture and get some spray. She brought in a can of room freshener and sprayed everywhere he told her to.

He was very tired when his daughter and I left at 8 p.m. that night, and he was ready to crawl into bed.

I arrived the next day while he was eating lunch and was told he had had another terrible night. He was quite tired and very quiet that Sunday afternoon. He was uncomfortable in his recliner, even after being settled in with a blanket and his radio. So, they put him in bed instead, and I left.

The aide had showered and shaved him when I got back at 4:45. As I walked into his room, he kept trying to get out of bed. He started swearing, using words I had never heard him say before. His swearing turned into screaming, accompanied by kicking and hitting. Five staff members and I tried to calm him down, but to no avail. They were finally able to get restraints on his ankles and tie his feet to the bed. He received an injection, which took about thirty minutes to take effect. Once he had calmed down, they untied his feet and bandaged two skinned elbows.

By 6:20, he was exhausted and calm. I didn't know if he was sound asleep or just half-awake, but I felt the need to talk to him about Jesus. I quietly told him that if he wanted to leave all these earthly problems and follow the light, it was okay. He was listening, and I wasn't expecting what happened next: he broke down and started to cry! His reaction took me by such surprise, I quickly added, "But you don't have to go anywhere if you don't want to; the decision is completely up to you." After shedding his last tear, he softly said to me, "I need to be closer to Jesus."

In order to lower the rate of his hallucinations, they needed to reduce the dose of a combination pill he was taking for Parkinson's. The drawback to this was that it would make his body stiffen up, which would lead to him being more bedridden. The thought of bringing him home in the condition he had been in the day before scared the life out of me.

When I saw him Monday morning, he was awake in bed and restless. He had been given a shot at six that morning because he was agitated when he woke up. He didn't want breakfast, so I ordered scrambled eggs and apple juice, but he didn't touch them, as he was asleep when they arrived. He slept a lot but was still able to converse when he was awake, although he never got out of bed.

He and I talked a lot about the Lord and Angels, and I felt we were on the same page. However, we never spoke again about dying, death, or his soon-to-come journey to Heaven.

Although his eating had almost ceased during the day, I ordered him a light dinner of chicken noodle soup, a dinner roll, two pats of butter, a fresh fruit cup, and a diet Sprite. He ate everything, and I went home at 5:45.

CHAPTER 09 | Going Home

It was Tuesday, November 9th, and Rick was scheduled to be discharged from the hospital. I arrived early and met with the doctor to discuss his transfer. Arrangements were made for a hospital bed, side table, and diapers to be delivered to the house at 12:30. Donna arrived in time to help with the transfer, and she stayed with her dad at the hospital while I returned home to receive the medical equipment.

As soon as I walked into the house, my phone rang. It was one of my grandsons calling to check on us. Little did he know, I was at my breaking point! As soon as I began to answer his question, I broke down in a flood of tears! He had no idea how much I needed that support from my family at that very moment, and the timing of his call was not a coincidence; it was perfect!

The doorbell rang, and the bed arrived. It was assembled quickly by an expert who had clearly put many beds together in his career. Everything was ready for Rick when he arrived home at 2:40 via ambulance, followed by Donna in her rental car.

An RN soon followed, bringing a package of diapers. She and I went over all of his medications. Six were discontinued, two were continued, and four more were added. The new pills were delivered while she and I were reviewing his schedule, though one was missing. She called the pharmacy, and they assured her it would arrive—and it did.

As soon as she left, I became Rick's full-time caregiver again. Everything had changed since he had left home nine days earlier, and I wasn't sure if I would be able to meet his needs. Donna was staying at a nearby hotel, which gave her some privacy and also gave Rick and me the chance to settle into a new routine.

I fixed his dinner, which consisted of poached eggs—one of his favorite foods, and easy for him to swallow. That memory of his first bite will stay with me forever! He closed his eyes and let out a sigh, "Mmmm!"

At first, it didn't seem like his wet diapers were going to be an issue. The first experience of getting him changed was chalked up to my inexperience! The first time was a challenge, but the second time was double the trouble. Similar to giving him a shower, we didn't work well together. By this time, he wasn't able to follow instructions, but he still insisted he knew how to do it and didn't think I knew anything!

By 10:15 that first night, he became quite agitated and was moving all around the bed. I found him beside the bed, trying to stand up. When I tried to maneuver him back up, he wouldn't budge, and suddenly flopped back down onto the bed in self-defeat; I was unable to move him further. So there he was.

Soon afterwards, I found him on the floor, unable to move or get up. It was useless to try to help him, so I dialed 9-1-1. They arrived within minutes and had him back in bed shortly after 11 p.m. I thought everything was under control—but not quite!

Nothing was going to stop him from trying to get out of that hospital bed. Even with the side rails up, which were only half the length of the bed, he was able to move his feet off. I got a chair and sat next to the bed, lifting his feet back up each time he tried to get out.

I didn't see it coming! Though he didn't have the strength to stand, he still had power. With one swift kick, I felt the sudden impact as I was halfway standing, trying to get his other leg back onto the bed. He kicked so hard, I lost my balance and went straight into the piano! With pain in my arm and tears in my eyes, I looked at him and said, "That really hurt!" With his energy completely drained, he just lay there, staring at the ceiling, unaware of what he had done. He showed no emotion at all—but at least he was still in bed!

I had already given Rick two very small doses of medicine that had come home with him, but it didn't even phase him. I no longer sat beside him, and the next time he tried to get out of bed, I called the Hospice nurse. When RN Marv arrived, he "talked" to Rick as he picked him up off the floor and put him back in bed.

Marv told me he would give Rick a larger dose of the same medicine and assured me it would still be safe. He stayed until Rick was sawing logs!

Rick woke up around 10:30 the next morning, and everything seemed calm, as if the night before had never happened. Donna was there, and Rick's aide arrived to give him a sponge bath and change the bed sheets. RN Sarah took his vitals and gave me another lesson in taking care of Rick. Each nurse had their own routines, and their suggestions were often a big help.

***

The next morning, Thursday, November 11th, RN Renee arrived. That was the day Rick got his catheter, which made my job so much easier! His son Jess had flown in from Oregon to say one last goodbye to his dad. He and Donna were staying at the same hotel, which was comforting—knowing they were close but had their own space.

The chaplain came as well and met with Donna, Jess, and me before visiting Rick to pray at his bedside. He seemed aware of the chaplain's presence, and as a Christian, Rick was receptive to the message that was given and the prayer that was said.

Hospice nurses and aides came every day, and their care was a huge relief for me. They weren't just there for Rick, but also provided the emotional support I so desperately needed. It became clear to me that I couldn't do it all alone now that Rick needed full care. I quickly realized how much worse "worse" could be!

The next day, November 12th, RN Sarah returned and changed the catheter bag, which was one duty I joyfully let her do! She noticed how dark and bloody his urine was—something I had noticed weeks earlier but hadn't recognized it as blood. I assumed the urine was too concentrated from not drinking enough water. She explained that its origin was unknown, as Rick had never been diagnosed with any condition that would cause bleeding. It was becoming harder for him to swallow pills, and his eating and drinking had significantly decreased. Sleeping took up most of his time.

I was encouraged to put a baby monitor in Rick's room, and was given many reasons why I would benefit from having one to keep a closer eye on him from another room in the house. In that moment, I agreed, and the new monitor arrived and was set up in his room. After all the company had gone, with only Rick and me spending quality time together, I didn't need the monitor and unplugged it. However, I realized it could definitely be useful if someone might want to monitor an individual remotely via their cell phone!

Between visitors, the days and evenings were quiet and peaceful with just the two of us. I played music on his Alexa—favorites like Josh Groban, Andy Williams, Roger Williams, Mantovani, Mancini, Ferrante & Teicher, and others. Knowing that hearing is the last sense to go, I read to him from *Guideposts*, prayed with him, and reminisced about earlier times we had enjoyed. Sometimes, I would sit beside his bed and read silently while he slept. I knew his days were numbered and wondered how much longer he could last, especially now that he wasn't even drinking water.

Donna's departure was a very sad one. She had given so much of herself to both of us during Rick's long journey. She always made time, despite her busy schedule, to provide the help and support we desperately needed and appreciated. I know she did it for her dad, and she will always be remembered as an Angel for what she did.

More family arrived on November 13th, and RN Carmen felt Rick only had twenty-four to forty-eight hours left. Lowering his Parkinson's medication caused his body to react unfavorably whenever he was moved, so his pain medication was increased and given more frequently.

Because of Rick's reaction to my earlier conversation in the hospital about giving him permission to be with the Lord, I never mentioned death, dying, or going to Heaven again. I realized how delicate the subject was for him, and I had no idea how he would respond if I brought it up again. It was so emotional for him that I decided it would be inappropriate and unappreciated for anyone else to feel they had the privilege to broach the subject—whether verbally, written, or read. I highly recommend that visitors choose their words carefully when speaking to someone in their final days.

One exception was with a friend experienced in divine healing and meditation. She asked if she could spend some time with Rick in those final hours to provide spiritual comfort and help him find peace. I welcomed her expertise and the offer to aid in his transition. He was asleep while she sat quietly and meditated.

On November 14th, Rick had a lot of company. Some visitors showed their emotions at his bedside, and I know he was able to hear everything happening around him. Furthermore, I have no doubt he recognized the voices he heard. I felt very protective of Rick and appreciated those who stayed calm in his presence. His breathing became labored that day, so RN Carmen adjusted his medication to reduce his anxiety.

His grandson, Walt, got emergency leave from North Carolina and, along with his mother (Rick's youngest daughter), arrived to pay their final respects.

Beth also brought Gidget for a last visit with Rick. Without opening his eyes, Rick knew his "Gidget baby" was smothering him with kisses, and he was as happy as he could be, feeling all that fur on his head. It was the closest he had come to a happy expression since eating his poached eggs! After Gidget settled down, she actually lay beside him on the bed and fell asleep.

Over the next few days, Rick's blood pressure gradually dropped. The nurses came every day, as promised. He started showing signs of congestion, but medication quickly got it under control. On the eighteenth, his urine became more sediment-filled, indicating his kidneys were beginning to shut down.

During those final days, I took the opportunity to ask him to forgive me for the times I had been impatient or agitated. There were moments when I undoubtedly had too much on my plate or was totally exhausted, and I wanted to clear the air. I also used that private time to let him know I forgave him for things only he and I knew about.

I recently watched *A Vow to Cherish* on TV and felt like I was part of that family. Feeling lonely does happen, but trusting the Lord is the only way to travel this journey with your loved one. My trust in the Lord kept me going through situations beyond my control. It was He who got me through all the yesterdays and He who would guide me through what was yet to come.

It was Friday evening, November 19th, and it had been a busy week with hospice coming every day. Rick looked very comfortable as he peacefully slept with his head resting on a soft pillow. Sitting beside his bed, I began telling him a story:

"Oh, Rick, look at that beautiful lake! Why, it's June Lake where you used to always go fishing with your buddies from work. Doesn't it make you want to get that old fishing pole out and put a worm on the end of the line so you can catch the biggest fish in the lake? The guys used to say you were the best fisherman they knew after you always caught the most or the biggest fish. Why, I remember when you used to love

fly fishing and spent hours making your own lures! When you got home from a fishing trip with the guys, you were already planning the next one.

Do you remember the trip when you drove that old VW Bus called "Buzz" all the way to June Lake with several of the guys riding with you? Everything went well until you started back down the hill coming home, and old Buzz died! You guys managed to find your way home, while Buzz got towed back to town!

The lake is huge, but I can see the shore way over on the other side. Hey Rick, someone is standing on that other shore waving their hands as if they see you. Who is it? Oh my gosh, Rick, it's your mom! She's at the lake, and I see her, and there's a little dog wagging his short stubby tail right next to her. You won't believe this, but it's Kurly Q!

Rick, do you see them? Your mom has Kurly Q, and she's motioning for you to come! Why don't you go to the other side and join them? You can take your magic pole and fish from there!"

It was about two o'clock in the morning, November 20, 2021, when I entered his room to check on him. With the soft light shining on his face, I could clearly see that he had gone fishing!

EPILOGUE

Rick stayed as long as he could but finally took the opportunity to go fishing again! I know his body is now perfect and pain-free once more, and I'm certain he wouldn't trade his new Heavenly life for the one he left behind.

During this long journey full of unknowns, I always knew God was in control and had a plan for both Rick and me. I communicated with the Lord daily, trusting Him to lead us in the right direction whenever we reached a crossroad, which happened many times.

The Lord knew exactly how, when, and where Rick's journey would end, and it was perfect. I am so thankful to have had those precious final days with him in the privacy of our home. I know he received the best care, I know his suffering was minimal, I know where he went, I know how he went, and I know he was surrounded by love.

Our son-in-law Jim officiated at Rick's funeral.

June sang "You'll Never Walk Alone" and "The Lord's Prayer." She was accompanied at the piano by her cousin and my friend, Jolene.

In another act of love, the other half of Kurly-Q's ashes were placed beside Rick's grave.